BERNICE

Echoes of Her Song in the Night

Bernice

Echoes of Her Song in the Night

Magna Boyes

Essence
PUBLISHING

Belleville, Ontario, Canada

BERNICE

Copyright © 2000, Magna Boyes

ISBN: 1-55306-100-4

Essence Publishing is a Christian Book Publisher dedicated to further-ing the work of Christ through the written word. For more information, contact: 44 Moira Street West, Belleville, Ontario, Canada K8P 1S3.
Phone: 1-800-238-6376. Fax: (613) 962-3055.
E-mail: info@essencegroup.com
Internet: www.essencegroup.com

Printed in Canada
by

Essence
PUBLISHING

DEDICATION

This book is dedicated to Bernice's fellow travelers who have a handicap in life's contest. A handicap usually refers to a competition in which difficulties are imposed or an advantage is given to contestants to equalize their chances.

For these travelers, the contest is life and the handicap ongoing. Sometimes just getting out of bed is a challenge.

God, who sees and understands everything, acknowledges with compassion the struggle to be and do in spite of limitations. His whispered "Well done" can be heard by those who listen for it.

Would that society recognize those who run with a handicap, see their potential, give advantage when needed and grade efforts on the curve. There are dividends for everyone.

"But the bravest are surely those who have the clearest vision of what is before them, glory and danger alike, and yet notwithstanding, go out and meet it" (Thucydides, 400 B.C.).

■ ■ ■

"Everything can be taken away from a man but one thing: the last of the human freedoms... to choose one's attitude in any given set of circumstances."

—Victor Frankl
(Austrian psychiatrist... a prisoner in Auschwitz)

"For I am persuaded, that neither death, nor life, nor angels, nor principalities, nor powers, nor things present, nor things to come, nor height, nor depth, nor any other creature, shall be able to separate us from the love of God, which is in Christ Jesus our Lord."

—Romans 8:38-39

TABLE OF CONTENTS

ACKNOWLEDGEMENTS

My sincere gratitude to family and friends who encouraged me in my mission to write Bernice's story; to Pam Hayes, Bernice's friend, for deciphering my handwritten manuscript; to Ellen Johnston who typed much of Bernice's early narrative; to Dr. John Gerrard for giving me access to Bernice's file; to David Nadeau for careful editing and much wise counsel; to Laura Ravndahl for navigating through the red pencil marks, keying in his corrections, searching out permissions in obscure places and producing a final printout beyond my dreams.

Thank You, my Heavenly Father, for giving me strength and courage to go on.

FOREWORD

The story of Bernice is a wonderful account of a young girl who overcame many physical difficulties and, in spite of them, maintained a radiant and positive outlook on life. Her Christian faith was an inspiration to all who knew her as a faithful witness for her Lord and Saviour Jesus Christ.

I am confident you will find renewed encouragement for life's journey; and those who struggle with a disability may see in Bernice a worthy role model.

It was my privilege as the family physician to attend at her birth and provide medical care for most of her life. As a member of my teen Sunday School class, she shared with us her gentle spirit and Christian grace. We are all better for having known her.

Dr. Fred T. Cenaiko

PREFACE

In the early winter months after Bernice's death, I began reading and organizing her writings. The volume overwhelmed me. It was all there, marking a progression of faith and work: notebooks of neat, handwritten meditations; pages of one-finger, typewritten narratives; then the more professional print from cousin Ellen's typewriter; and finally, the unmistakable stamp of Bernice's computer.

These pages revealed the growing and maturing of her soul. Should these writings be stored in boxes on the top shelf of my closet? No, for Bernice lived and wrote with the keen desire to share God's love and to glorify Him. But how could I take up the torch and light a flame to fulfill her dream?

About that time, *Reader's Digest* featured a story about a family's struggle with illness. After years of treatments, hopes dashed and revived again, the invalid daughter said to her mother, "This has been an experience of courage and faith. It should be told to help others. You can do it, Mom!"

Her statement zapped me like a bolt from heaven. I decided that with God enabling me, I would not allow Bernice's story to gather dust in my closet. With a mother's determination, I started organizing.

Bernice was shy. She related well individually, but group socializing often left her tongue-tied. Agonizing over this in her teen years, she let off steam in her diary: "If anyone else asks why I am so quiet, I shall react in an uncharacteristic way!" The caption under her yearbook grad picture carries a variation on the same theme: "Quiet people aren't the only ones who don't say much."

She had a lot to say and share. In her heart resided a wealth of learned wisdom, deep spiritual understanding and love. She shared it with some who were her close friends, but through her computer she poured out her longings, hurts, defeats, victories and hopes. In her early twenties, she wrote an autobiography, the story of her struggles. She called it *Song in the Night*. It was added to, deleted from and revised many times. Dispatched to publishers time and again, it was returned, "Sorry, this manuscript does not meet our present needs." Deeply disappointed, she turned her attention to other ways of expressing her feelings. Excerpts from her autobiography and other writings appear in this book.

Hear her voice, echoes of her songs in the night.

E arly in the morning of November 24, 1995, the telephone rang in our Birch Hills home.

"This is the Regina General Hospital. We have your daughter, Bernice, here. She is not breathing."

"Is there anything you can do?"

"We are trying. She may have aspirated something. She is not responding."

"Do the best you can. I'll come as soon as possible."

Dear Jesus, how can that frail little frame endure this trauma? Those small struggling lungs? Hold her, Jesus, in Your hands. She's in Your care now. You are the Great Physician. You make the decision, Lord, for You know the plans You have for her.

I phoned her uncle and aunt in Regina, Jim and Margaret Brown, to go to emergency. Millie Rowluck agreed to take me to Regina, a four-hour drive from Birch Hills. It was dark and snowing. We could only pray and wait patiently, though my mind raced ahead with desperate yearning and foreboding. *Please God, she's in Your hands. You brought her through many a crisis before. We need a miracle now. Without a miracle can she endure this trauma? Don't let her suffer, Lord. If this is the end of her journey, please take her gently home.*

As the hours passed, I talked and prayed with Millie. I recalled promises that had sustained us before. "Fear not, for I am with thee: be not dismayed, for I am thy God; I will strengthen thee, yea, I will help thee" (Isa. 41:10).

Fear. Bernice was no stranger to fear. Living in a body which had more than once threatened to collapse, she learned to live one day at a time by God's grace. She had the Bible on her computer and, with the touch of a finger, could summon pages of "fear not" promises. She pinned them to the wall and noted them as she passed by in her wheelchair. Other times the theme on the wall spoke of "trusting" or "standing firm." She often marveled at the grace of God—how many things could go wrong, but didn't. She had so little pain, her doctors were amazed.

We arrived at the hospital. In my heart I knew she was gone. We were directed to emergency and waited in a quiet room for the doctor. The Browns had come as I had requested, but had already left. A doctor came in and told us they had not been able to revive Bernice. He said he was sorry and allowed us to see her.

She was lying on a stretcher in a quiet side room, wearing that familiar night shirt with the teddy bears on it.

So small. So small. Only sixty-two pounds. *This time, my sweetheart, your guardian angel took you home. In your thirty-one years you have been spared so many calamities, but this time it was a call to "come home, good and faithful servant."*

You were always afraid of choking, having had more than one scary experience. Thinking of the future, you trembled a little, but clung to Him who has a plan for us: "For I know the plans I have for you, declares the Lord, plans to prosper you and not to harm you, plans to give you hope and a future" (Jer. 29:11, NIV). Surely the future He speaks of reaches beyond the grave. You exceeded doctors' expectations for your life, but God's expectations continue into eternity.

Your own plans, my sweetheart, were fabulous. What you accomplished in spite of difficulties is a series of miracles. Your mind teemed with plans, ideas and dreams... all of them to help others and honour the Lord. Some were fulfilled, many were not. Your body could not keep up. Had it been possible, I would have traded places to give you a chance to live your dreams. But the Lord's plan is fulfilled in you. Now you know that. Now you are free and rejoicing because you see the end from the beginning. We still "see through a glass darkly" here, but one day we shall rejoice together. Thank you for the time we shared on earth. You were a gift beyond measure.

We stood beside her, stroked her hair, held her hands. I kissed her cheek over and over. The last time, only a few days before, when I visited with her at Wascana Rehabilitation Centre, I didn't kiss her good-bye because I had a cold! Germs. What do they matter? These are regrets, but she has forgiven me, sweet, gentle soul that she is. Can I forgive myself? I must, or life will be intolerable.

CHAPTER ONE

In the Beginning

Tom Boyes returned from Europe after the war to resume farming near Domremy, Saskatchewan. He and his family were longtime friends of mine. My plans were to go to South Africa with TEAM. In 1957, after one term at a missionary children's home, I returned to Canada, and we were married the following year. Growing grain and raising cattle kept us happily busy for many years.

In 1961, we adopted a one-year-old, brown-eyed boy, Brian David. A sweet, gentle child, he adjusted remarkably well to his new situation. He and Tom spent all available time together. Horses and cattle fascinated him. It was almost a rite of passage to come in with manure on his boots. He loved to "help." When Tom washed at the sink, Brian stood on a stool beside him, imitating every move. All farmers have a snooze after dinner. They would share a cushion on the kitchen floor for ten minutes. Tom snoozed and Brian lay quietly, eyes wide open, waiting patiently for the next activity.

One of Brian's favourite toys, a farm site complete with barn, machinery and livestock, reinforced his preoccupation with the barnyard. On stormy days he continued his farm activity on our kitchen table. Under his chubby hand, the John Deere tractor delivered hay to the cows and helped clean the barn. He could imitate perfectly the putt-putt-putt sound of the tractor.

On April 15, 1964, a baby sister, Bernice Sarah, was born. Brian went to Grandma and Grandpa Harstad's for a few days, and when Tom brought Brian home, he looked at his new sister for a long time. "She's small," he said. Too small to play properly, but it wasn't long before she joined him at the kitchen table in her recliner seat. As time went by and Bernice became floor-mobile, they found more sharing things to do together.

When Bernice was born, we noticed her big toes were turned inward, giving her feet a bunion look. We also noticed that as she lay on one side for a while, her head appeared flat on that side. This disappeared as she turned to the other side. The doctor had no explanation. The swellings would reappear, and at times her head seemed larger than normal. Our family physician, Dr. Fred Cenaiko, referred us to Dr. John Gerrard, professor of Pediatrics at University Hospital in Saskatoon. We saw him in September when Bernice was five months old. They checked family history, gave Bernice a thorough physical and took X-rays of her head. A possible diagnosis—hydrocephalus. Something was wrong, but they couldn't identify it.

We took her home and tried to go on with life as normally as possible. *God, You gave us a baby girl. We thank You for her. We love her. Whatever happens, we trust Your judgment.* There were tears shed, but laughter too, as Bernice developed normally, smiled and learned to talk. Brian accepted her as a playmate who crawled on the floor and laughed at his antics. They both enjoyed Sunday School and clapped vigorously as they sang. We appreciated the concern and prayers of the Wakaw Baptist Church congregation.

We saw the doctor again in December, 1965, after Bernice developed a swelling on her forehead after a fall. Both eyes were swollen, but no definite diagnosis was made. In March, 1966, we noticed a walnut-sized lump at the base of her neck. Pink and tender, it spread around her neck and to her shoulders. She couldn't raise her arms. Back to Saskatoon and Dr. Gerrard. There were consultations. Several doctors were discussing an article in the *Lancet Medical Journal.* Dr. Gerrard turned to us and said, "Your daughter has a rare condition called *myositis ossificans progressiva.* We don't know the cause and there is no treatment. It involves calcification of the muscles and spreads to other parts of the body. It causes severe crippling as time goes on. I am sorry. We will do all we can to find information that might help."

It was a heavy sentence. We looked at our little blonde angel. She was unaware of the judgment that had just been pronounced on her future. What lay in store for her? For us? Our emotions were numb. Our hearts cried out to God. *Please help us.* Later, we had some serious conversations with Him.

"What have You in mind, Lord? We know You have plans for Your children. We have plans too. We didn't count on anything like this. Now we have been cast completely on Your mercy. We have to ask why because we don't know. Do we need to know? It would help—maybe. You do have a plan, don't You, Lord? These are not just chance happenings along the way, are they? You are aware of us, aren't You? We read that all things work together for good to those who love You. We have to trust You because You are our lifeline, our only source for this life and the next. Help us, Lord, to take one day at a time. How else can we cope?"

It was a one-way conversation for a long time. There were attacks of panic, desperate pleas, floods of tears. Then He answered.

"I have loved thee with an everlasting love: therefore with loving kindness have I drawn thee" (Jer. 31:3).

"When thou passest through the waters, I will be with thee; and through the rivers, they shall not overflow thee: when thou walkest through the fire, thou shalt not be burned... (Isa. 43:2).

"My grace is sufficient for thee, for my strength is made perfect in weakness (2 Cor. 12:9).

"Trust in the Lord with all thy heart; and lean not unto thine own understanding. In all thy ways acknowledge Him, and He shall direct thy paths (Prov. 3:5-6).

"But they that wait upon the Lord shall renew their strength; they shall mount up with wings as eagles; they shall run, and not be weary, and they shall walk and not faint" (Isa. 40:31).

"For I know the plans I have for you, declares the Lord, plans to prosper you and not to harm you, plans to give you hope and a future" (Jer. 29:11, NIV).

"Cast thy burden upon the Lord, and He shall sustain

thee..." (Ps. 55:22).

"Let not your heart be troubled; you believe in God, believe also in Me. In My Father's house are many mansions.... I go to prepare a place for you.... I will come again and receive you to Myself, that where I am, there you may be also.... I am the way, the truth and the life" (John 14:1-4,6, NKJV).

Thank You, Lord. We trust You.

"I will lift up mine eyes unto the hills, from whence cometh my help. My help cometh from the Lord, which made heaven and earth" (Ps. 121:1-2).

"I can do all things through Christ which strengtheneth me" (Phil. 4:13).

"Now we see through a glass, darkly; but then, face to face: now I know in part; but then shall I know even as also I am known" (1 Cor. 13:12).

We knew then what we were facing. We knew, too, that God's strength and wisdom were available to us. Dr. Gerrard's promise of help comforted us. Indeed, over the years we developed a friendly rapport with him, as we consulted about problems. He and Bernice often exchanged cheerful notes and birthday cards.

We soon realized that even the slightest injury would trigger instant swelling. How could we protect a toddler from falling?

Not easy! I sewed a harness with long straps at the back. That summer, Carol Sollid and a neighbour, Willamine, came to help. They followed Bernice everywhere, keeping a tight rein! This proved exhausting to the former and frustrating to the latter. Would a helmet add more protection and freedom? We tried it with good success. Bernice used that helmet until she was twelve.

Brother Brian suffered his own frustrations. We tried not to be paranoid about Bernice's safety, but it showed. Can you play, really play, when so much caution must be observed? As time passed, we adjusted to the situation, and a certain circumspect calm pervaded the household.

At times, the calm cracked. At breakfast one morning, I glanced at Tom and saw tears running down his cheeks. He turned away for a moment, then looked back and joined Bernice and the rest of us in small talk. How often our hearts were lifted by her cheerful nature.

True to his word, Dr. Gerrard sought advice from every possible source regarding Bernice's disorder. He sent letters to the Hospital for Sick Children in Toronto, the Mayo Clinic in Rochester, Minnesota, University Hospital in Edmonton, the Children's Orthopedic Hospital in Seattle and the University of Wisconsin.

In each case, the response was the same. "Our experience with this disease is very limited. For this reason no one is interested in pursuing research. There is no helpful treatment we can recommend."

Back to square one. Dr. Gerrard, Dr. Cenaiko and ourselves embarked on a three-way collaboration to keep Bernice as well as possible.

She was admitted to Saskatoon University Hospital in March, 1966, for tests and X-rays.

They discharged her on diminishing doses of steroids. Dr. Gerrard saw her again in May. His comment: "She is a pink, cheerful child in no distress, but with great limitation of movement in the neck, spine and shoulders."

The prednisone failed to alleviate the increasing stiffness in her shoulders. Bernice couldn't lift her arms enough to feed herself, scratch her nose or protect herself when she fell. The helmet helped.

We went home and settled into a new mode of living, while carefully maintaining communication with Dr. Gerrard.

October 8, 1966—appointment

"A pale but cheerful child whose neck is virtually fixed, who can hardly move her arms, and whose elbows are fixed at a right angle. She cannot bend her trunk or rise from a sitting position. Movements in the hips, knees, ankles, fingers and wrists are still full. Two boney nodules are present over the scapulae." (JWG)

December 31, 1966—appointment

"Bernice's myositis ossificans has not progressed in the interim, and movement at the shoulders and neck is greater than two months ago. She can look readily in all directions. The wrists, fingers, hips, knees and ankles are as yet unaffected. Several calcified lumps are present on the back. It is probable that during the course of the next year or two the skin over these lumps will erode and deposits of calcium will be extruded. The parents were warned of this." (JWG) (This never happened in her thirty-one years. Thank God!)

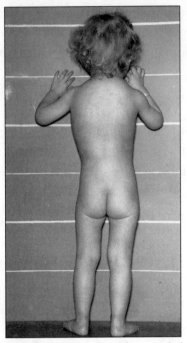

Swelling spreading over the shoulders and down the back
from initial lesion at the base of the neck.

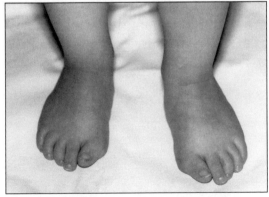

Deformity of great toes a significant symptom
of myositis ossificans.

CHAPTER TWO

The Venezuela Experiment

Bernice's Aunt Dorothy was a missionary in Venezuela. Early in 1967, she wrote with a startling proposal. She knew a doctor there who treated patients successfully with unconventional methods. When she told him about Bernice's disease, he felt optimistic about helping her, so Dorothy urged us to come.

Aunt Anna was home on leave from her missionary work in Kenya. She would stay with Tom and Brian, and I would take three-year-old Bernice to Venezuela. It was a scary thought, but we were motivated. Could we pass up a possible chance of help for Bernice?

We flew from Saskatoon to Toronto, then to New York. Waiting at Kennedy Airport for our flight to Caracas was a harrowing experience. Tired and frustrated, Bernice refused to walk. She cried. She wet her pants. Finally, we were off. Someone drew our attention to the lights of Puerto Rico and other points of interest, but we were not excited. The lights of Caracas did wake us up. We stepped out into the 80 degree temperature of Caracas with our "light" winter apparel. What a shock! Such a drastic change. Were we still on planet earth?

Dorothy, who lived some distance away, had alerted missionary friends to meet us. What a relief to see them. We gratefully shed our stuffy clothing and relaxed in their hospitality. Bernice slept well, but I must have eaten something unfriendly on the plane. Most of the night was spent in the bathroom. Bernice seemed quite overwhelmed by all the new sights and sounds. She didn't say much, but as we stood on the balcony surveying the city, she suddenly burst out singing "O Canada!" Yes, our home and native land did seem rather far away.

The next day, we flew in a small plane over rugged, forested hills until the rooftops of Barquisimeto glinted in the sun. We had arrived safely, thank God. Bernice and I shared a double bed, no doubt vacated by Deborah, Dorothy's co-worker, who slept in a hammock on the patio.

The house exhibited a typical local appearance: barred windows for security, polished red wax floors and painted walls. After supper, the dishes were washed, scalded and placed in a covered rack on the kitchen table. To foil mice, Deborah told us. She prepared us for wildlife in the house. The mat in the shower was shaken to scare away cockroaches. We learned that amoebae are likely to inhabit certain vegetables, but Dorothy had refused to give up her salads. She soaked the lettuce in potassium permanganate. We declined every uncooked item except bananas and oranges. Dorothy graciously put up with our phobias.

We experienced a missionary's daily responsibilities: conducting children's classes on patios everywhere, using portable flannel boards to display the figures of Bible stories. Church services were long and lively. The Spanish language bypassed us completely, but music struck a familiar note so we sang along in English and followed the Scripture reading in our English Bible. The Lord Jesus, who knows every language and every heart, blessed us all.

Shops and business places opened early and closed early during the hot season. Beaches and pools attracted young and old. We spent time on our shaded patio.

When the time came to visit the doctor, we travelled many kilometers on hot, winding roads. Finally there, we sat in his austere waiting room, I the only one tight-lipped and fighting apprehension. *We're in Your hands, Lord.* Blood and urine tests were ordered, as well as X-rays. Eventually we found ourselves in his office. He examined Bernice and we talked at length. He concluded that her disorder was not what he had in mind. However, he felt medication would improve her general well-being and could even affect the progress of the disease. Bernice would receive half an ampule, according to her size. Dorothy comforted me by taking the other half!

As near as we could understand, the principle behind this treatment is a sort of chain reaction aeration which attacks any pathology in the body. In Bernice's case, her calcium deposits did not fit the usual picture of pathology. Admittedly, we were disappointed, though we knew from the beginning it was a slim chance.

Time for a conversation with God again.

"We asked for guidance, Lord, and we came. Is it a total wild goose chase? You knew this treatment is not specific for Bernice's disorder. We didn't, so we had to try. Maybe it will help a little. We have to trust You. The Apostle

Peter, when faced with a crucial decision, said, 'Lord, to whom (else) shall we go? Thou hast the words of eternal life. And we believe and are sure that thou art the Christ, the Son of the living God' (John 6:68-69). We stand on that foundation. Keep us in the hollow of Your hand, heavenly Father."

After a sleepless night and a few tears, He answered.

"Peace I leave with you, my peace I give unto you.... Let not your heart be troubled" (John 14:27).

"Fear thou not; for I for I am with thee: be not dismayed; for I am thy God: I will strengthen thee; yea, I will help thee" (Isa. 41:10).

"Faith is the assurance of things hoped for, the conviction of things not seen" (Heb. 11:1, NAS).

"The Lord is my shepherd; I shall not want" (Psalm 23:1).

"The Lord is good, a stronghold in the day of trouble; and He knoweth them that trust in Him" (Nah. 1:7).

"I will both lay me down in peace, and sleep: for thou, Lord, only makest me dwell in safety" (Ps. 4:8).

The doctor suggested we travel to Canada by surface transportation rather than fly because he thought the difference in atmospheric pressure might affect the performance of Bernice's medication. We felt obliged to comply, even though it was more difficult and time consuming. Bernice and Dorothy celebrated birthdays in April with cake and token gifts. We sailed from Puerto Cabello on a freighter, April 13, 1967. About twenty passengers, mostly Americans, settled in for a pleasant cruise to Baltimore. The legendary blue Caribbean was calm, but the scene changed when we headed into the Atlantic. At suppertime, the ship suddenly lurched to starboard, taking food, furniture and passengers in the same direction. I grabbed Bernice from her chair and clung to the table, which was bolted to the floor. A steward supported us until the rolling subsided. Whew! Recounting this incident years later, Bernice took great delight in describing my reaction. "Mom thought we had strayed into the Bermuda Triangle and could be sucked down into Davey Jones locker." *Au contraire!* At that point, we would part company with the ship and go up instead of down. Our Lord has prepared a place for us up there.

The sea remained grey and choppy all the way to Baltimore. Bernice wanted to be up and about, climbing over barricades, peeking through the railings. *Dear Jesus, she'll need that determination and will power in years to come.*

With the last leg of the journey in sight, we boarded a bus in Baltimore for Toronto. There, we enjoyed a brief respite with Sue and Les Elliott, Bernice's aunt and uncle. Then, off by train to Saskatoon where Tom and Brian met us. *O Saskatchewan, how I love thee; let me count the ways. Home, sweet home and dear familiar faces. Thank You, Jesus.*

All of life's experiences teach us something if we don't clog the channel with a sour attitude. If we are convinced God is ultimately in charge of His willful, headstrong children, we can navigate among the rose gardens and land mines of life with a measure of equanimity.

"O Lord, You have searched me and known me. You know my sitting down and my rising up; You understand my thought afar off. You comprehend my path and my lying down, and are acquainted with all my ways. For there is not a word on my tongue, but behold, O Lord, You know it altogether. You have hedged me behind and before, and laid Your hand upon me" (Ps. 139:1-5, NKJV).

Dr. Gerrard kept his own counsel about the usefulness of our trip to Venezuela. Medically speaking, it seemed unproductive, but who knows the inner workings of God's plans? Time, and certainly eternity, will reveal things hidden from us now.

We settled into a "life goes on" mode. Brian had started school, riding the bus twelve miles to Crystal Springs. Aunt Anna was substitute teaching for a few weeks so they travelled together. Bernice wore her helmet and dutifully chewed her vitamins. In July, 1967, Dr. Gerrard referred us to the Department of Rehabilitation to check out the possibility of an exercise program for Bernice's arms and fingers. The use of her hands to eat and play seemed to encourage mobility.

Pastor Ridgway, on one of his visits, gently broached another subject for our consideration. Kathryn Khulman, a faith healer, would visit Vancouver in the fall. Would we be interested in taking Bernice to her meetings? He had friends there, Bill and Winnie Pegg, with whom we could stay. As we talked and prayed at length, Tom wondered about the wisdom of another long trip, but I felt strongly motivated to go. Bernice, then past four years, agreed that we must not miss this opportunity. "In case God has arranged this for us," she said.

Winnie met us at the airport. She and Bill prayed with us as we prepared our hearts for the service the next day. "Here we are again, Lord, coming with humble hearts before the Great Physician to ask a blessing from You. We stand in awe of You, all wise, all powerful, for we are so finite. You see our need, we ask Your help."

We stood in line at the arena with hundreds of others, waiting for the doors to open. Several people brushed past us. We were startled to see Kathryn Khulman. She smiled and patted Bernice's head as she walked by. Inside, we sat near the front, part of a crowd of thousands, all waiting for God's touch. Many were called to come forward to report their healing. Should we go forward or wait to be called? We struggled with the decision. We sat and prayed, waiting for God to find us where we were. We knew He could see us. Much later, we went home with our friends, feeling a little disappointed. No visible change could be seen in Bernice. Yet as we talked, a quiet peace filled our hearts. All is well because the Lord is here.

"Peace I leave with you; my peace I give unto you.... Let not your heart be troubled" (John 14:27).

We read this verse to mean God was saying, "Trust Me. I am still here. Let Me work out My plan for you. One day you will see the reason for everything." *Thank You, Lord.*

The next day, we took a taxi to visit Aunt Alice and Uncle Harry. After supper they brought us back. In the course of the evening we talked of many things... life, death and the purpose of God in everything. Aunt Alice, who many years ago had let her faith be side-tracked, struggled to remember the sure Word she once knew so well. Harry admitted he had never given much thought to spiritual matters, but if indeed it is possible to know forgiveness of sin in Jesus Christ, he wanted that assurance. With encouragement from us all, he began a journey of faith which slowly blossomed. Alice, new life revived in her heart, became his encourager.

Bernice and I flew home, feeling satisfied and at peace with our journey, thankful for new friends, Bill and Winnie, and praising God for His evident work in Alice and Harry.

On a subsequent family visit to Vancouver, we experienced another gentle word of encouragement from the Lord. Touring the town with Alice, we found a restaurant where we could rest and revive. Bernice, peering out from under her helmet, had great fun with the menu. In the midst of our merriment, two men strolled by and stopped at our booth. They smiled and made a few comments. One placed his hand on Bernice's head and said, "This child will be a blessing and inspiration to all of you." Then they walked away.

Thank You, Lord, for reminding us that You have a plan. We will trust You.

CHAPTER THREE

School Days

Bernice quickly picked up new and useful information from Brian's workbooks. "Sesame Street" and "Mr. Dress-up" taught daily from the television, and we read books by the hour. But as Bernice's sixth birthday approached, we knew something had to be done about school. She wanted to go.

We discussed the situation with the superintendent and Crystal Springs school staff. It would mean a long ride on the bus, plus the rough and tumble of school life. A few adjustments were made. Hobey, the bus driver, would drive into our yard. Someone would be designated to take Bernice to the school washroom downstairs. It was settled. She could hardly wait for fall! In anticipation, I experienced some fear and trembling. *Dear Jesus, dispatch a guardian angel to travel with her.*

The day came, September, 1970. Helmet on, lunch box in hand, she boarded the bus. She sat near the window so she wouldn't slide off the seat on turns. Those were my instructions. If she ever slid into the aisle, she didn't tell me. Every day became an adventure. She made friends and joined in every activity. Learning was an exciting challenge. She loved her teacher, Mrs. MacFie. As it turned out, it was the teacher who took her to the washroom quite often. Much later, when everyone used the modern facilities in the senior department, her friend Val became her helper.

From Bernice's diary, her own estimate of those days:

"My early school days were more or less normal, under the circumstances. I went through the everyday traumas of childhood: falling off the swing, skinning knees, breaking my nose, breaking my glasses."

Bernice gloried in being "just like the other kids." Aside from her disability, she had an idea or two that were different. Her teacher told me Bernice wanted to start a Sunday School class for her classmates. This was in grade two. The plan didn't get off the ground; the teacher felt the children needed to play outside at noon. So Bernice earned (at an early age) the friendly nick-name, "Rev. Boyes."

Practicing for field day presented another challenge. We raved over the news—she made 13.4 feet in the hop-step-and-jump. She ran the half-mile in the inside lane. Others cheered her on as they passed.

When the band was organized in the fall, the instruments were carefully scrutinized for possibilities. Bernice signed up for drums. Sadly, this proved to be out of reach for her so she had a choice of glockenspiel or the triangle. Brian was in the senior band, playing trombone. The band continued for several years with great promise, but when the bandmaster was transferred, no replacement could be found.

Every fall and spring we travelled to Briercrest Bible College for the missions conference and graduation respectively. We enjoyed the hospitality of Aunt Beatrice and Uncle Arthur Sundbo. These were treasured visits where we received strength for body and soul. Always on the agenda were great preaching and beautiful music. Aunt Beatrice took Bernice to the children's sessions.

One afternoon she confided to us, "I stood up for Jesus today. They asked who wants Jesus to be your Saviour. Some kids put up their hands. They didn't see me so I stood up. I guess Jesus saw me anyway, but I wanted everybody to see me." She was five.

From that day, Bernice was convinced Jesus had seen her and that she belonged to Him. Because she wanted to share that good news with others, she looked for opportunities, not only to speak for Jesus, but to be kind. Quick to spot children who had problems, who were left out or ridiculed, she was drawn to them. We had many conversations at home about these situations.

"She's a nice girl, Mom, but some of the kids don't like her. I feel sorry for her." "Then you be her friend, Bernice. Jesus loves us all, so we must show love too." A bumper sticker expresses a philosophy that developed early in Bernice's life: "Commit random acts of kindness and senseless acts of beauty."

There was a reckless spontaneity about some of the ideas birthed in her heart. As they were translated into action through her hands and lips, her selfless spirit blossomed with age. She learned to delegate some of the action to others and knew how to inspire others to see her vision. "We're a team, right, Mom?"

There were notes of encouragement, birthday gifts, no-special-occasion gifts, visits, parties, prayers, phone calls, more parties. Classmates and friends arrived on the bus for her birthday, often on separate days to accommodate everyone. She, in turn, helped others celebrate. The happy face became her signature on all communications.

She conspired with a neighbour friend, Kathy, to organize anniversary parties for both sets of parents. These were elaborate affairs complete with cake, balloons, gifts and candles. Gala as they were, these outings often ended in tears when it was time to go home. Bernice and Kathy were close pals. Their friendship survived the changes that passing years bring; Kathy entered the work force, got married and became a mother. They still arranged a rendezvous whenever possible.

For several years, the annual February "Youth Quake" at Caronport was on our agenda. We brought three or four teens in our station wagon to be part of the 1,000 plus young people who attended the retreat. Bernice couldn't participate in the weekend's strenuous activities, but on one occasion, when she was sixteen, her entry in the poetry contest won a prize. She limped to the podium to recite her lines and receive a Briercrest T-shirt.

God's Creation

One day as I stood on the sun-swept plain
and walked past the trees, still soaked with rain;
One day as I stopped and pondered with awe
at the God-made beauty in all that I saw;
One day as I watched the babbling stream
that sparkled and danced with a jubilant gleam,
Far on the horizon were cattle and sheep
grazing on hills that lay soundly asleep.

I wondered and wondered how men could believe
that any but God could possibly weave
such beauty, such majesty into this world.
Before me, the glory of God was unfurled;
No more do I wonder why most people find
This miracle just happened... it's because they are blind.
Lord, may the light of Your purpose and plan
Dawn in the hearts of misguided man.

■ ■ ■

The prairie wind posed a problem for Bernice, often snatching away her short supply of breath. Once, we were walking to the Caronport gym for morning service. Tom held his jacket to shield her face, but it wasn't enough. She panicked. Tom quickly carried her to a nearby dorm where they waited in the entrance until Bernice regained her breath. "Dad! This is the girls' dorm! You're not supposed to be here!" Dad, having lived long and survived much, didn't react in any perceptible way to this announcement. We continued our trek to the gym, the jacket over Bernice's head.

Over the years, many earnest prayers had been offered for Bernice's healing. God heard and answered in ways not always apparent to us at the time. We felt His presence with us. An excerpt from Bernice's writings:

"It would take both hands and all ten toes to count the number of times someone has prayed for my physical healing, and every time God says, 'Not yet.' I believe some day God will heal my body. Folks say to me, 'You need more faith.' But I'm trusting God. When the time comes, Jesus will reach down and perform His miracle. He prepares the way before me and I will be ready for it. And if

He chooses not to heal me while I'm a resident of earth, I'll be running down the streets of heaven in my own marathon. So whether my body straightens out or remains the same, I'm still a winner. I've received the greatest miracle of all... the healing of my spirit, the inner me. Because of that I can live above the restrictions of my 'outer shell.' Here's a neat saying: 'God can use a crooked stick to draw a straight line.'"

As months passed, Bernice's condition stabilized, and she adjusted to her limitations. Her arms were fixed, held in front of her chest, though the wrists and fingers were mobile. Because her back was rigid, she would fall like a tree, unable to help herself. Thankfully, this did not happen very often. She learned to retrieve things from the floor by getting right down on her knees. "No problem," she said.

We maintained close contact with the doctors. Bernice was scheduled for a pulmonary function study. Her chest muscles were becoming calcified and unyielding. After one experience with pneumonia, we received a standing order for penicillin. On one of our trips to University Hospital in Saskatoon, we participated in the grand rounds. How Bernice enjoyed talking to the medical students and answering questions.

We had noticed for some time that Bernice appeared to be developing a tilt to the right. We added a riser under her right shoe, hoping to counteract this trend. When we consulted Dr. Gerrard, he wrote:

Dear Mr. and Mrs. Boyes: *June, 1974*
Many thanks for your letter. I was sorry to hear that Bernice is developing a tilt, and that her left arm is beginning to rub

against her body and cause a sore spot.

I am sure the calcification in her muscles is fixing her spine at a tilt and not in a straight line. I do not think it is possible to correct the tilt by surgery, but wonder if it might not be possible to prevent it becoming worse by watching the position she adopts when asleep. While asleep, does she tend to lie with a kink in her right side? If she does, then any calcification in the muscles would tend to fix the body in this position. If so, perhaps she could be persuaded to sleep in another position.

Do congratulate her on jumping so far in the hop, skip and jump.

We would be happy to see Bernice at any time, should you wish.

In the spring of 1976, Bernice turned twelve and had completed grade six in style. To celebrate, we planned a holiday to Vancouver to visit Aunt Alice. Tom and Brian finished the farm spring work, turned the cattle out to pasture, and we were off. With Alice we investigated every point of interest, from the heights in cable cars to seaside strolls among the roses. Tom's brother Stanley and family lived in Duncan, so we experienced a ferry trip to the island.

Returning to Vancouver on the ferry, Bernice noticed her leg was sore when she sat on the hard seats. By the time we were due to fly home, her left leg was swollen and tender. The villain had struck again.

Dr. Cenaiko's X-ray verified that the myositis ossificans was mounting a fresh attack. We treated her symptomatically, with Tylenol™ and tender loving care. Gradually, the swelling subsided, but more calcification left her hip and knee so restricted she couldn't sit properly. She insisted on hobbling about, and we feel this kept some mobility in her leg.

Bernice raised the question: What about school? Obviously, she could not ride the bus or sit in regular school seats, so after further consultations with the superintendent and the teachers, some firm plans were made. Mr. Klassen, who taught grades seven and eight, would supply us with textbooks and notes, and he would check her work and allow her to write exams at home. Mom and Dad, with some help from Pastor and Mrs. Ridgway, became teachers. Aunt Anna arrived from Kenya in time to supervise grade eight. Bernice knelt on a pillow beside her bed, or sat briefly on a stool. All systems were go.

We once had a dog which lost a leg in a mishap. We were devastated for him, but before long his speed was up to par and the light returned to his eyes. Bernice felt a kinship with him. Though left with a permanent limp, she became amazingly agile and stable.

With grade eight exams under her belt, she was on cloud nine. "I'm going to make it, praise the Lord!" The home support team applauded themselves for a job well done. We could not rest on our laurels too long, as different plans were needed for grade nine. Harley Sundbo, the superintendent, arranged for a tutor to come to our home twice a week. Louise Wick, a part-time teacher who lived nearby, agreed to take it on. This happy collaboration continued for four years. Correspondence courses were ordered from Regina, and the local school supplied textbooks and hands-on instruction in lab work. These lab trips maintained contact with Bernice's classmates, a vital part of her mental and emotional development. She was thrilled to keep up with her class, though on a parallel track.

In February, 1977, Aunt Beatrice passed away after a long struggle with cancer. We were reluctant to part with her, who had loved us all and prayed for us so faithfully. Four children had preceded her to heaven. In her book, *Treasures in Heaven*, she wrote, "God did not take you children from us. He keeps you for us. We know we will see all of you again in our Saviour's presence... when the morning breaks and the shadows flee away." The Word of God spoke peace to Uncle Art during those lonely days. He shared those promises with Bettie, his eldest daughter, and her family, treasures left to bless him on his continuing journey.

"Eye hath not seen, nor ear heard, neither have entered into the heart of man, the things which God hath prepared for them that love him" (1 Cor. 2:9).

Bernice's left elbow presented a problem. Due to the aggravated tilt of her torso, the elbow developed a tender area from contact with clothing and skin. Should this become infected, there was danger of bone involvement. Dr. Cenaiko and Dr. Silver suggested breaking the humerus surgically in order to raise the elbow away from the body. We were fearful of this procedure because Bernice's limited lung capacity presented some danger of pneumonia, and the trauma of surgery could trigger further flare-ups of her disease. Bernice came to a decision: "I'll just trust the Lord. He's looking after me."

We needed to find some other way to relieve pressure on her elbow. When referred to the Children's Rehabilitation Centre, Bernice was assessed by a social worker, a physiotherapist, an occupational therapist, a speech therapist, a nurse and a doctor.

Someone from the Council for Crippled Children and Adults fashioned a device from a child's blood pressure cuff. The bulb hung over her shirt at the neck so she could pump it up as necessary. It deflated at night, however, when it was most needed, so we eventually had to settle for a folded sanitary napkin. We were concerned that long use would create a depression in Bernice's chest, but as the lesser of two evils, it proved quite satisfactory in the long term. After the sore area healed, we kept a piece of cloth there to separate the two areas of skin... a space of only .05 centimeters. As Bernice said, the Lord looked after her. They measured her for a reinforced foam seat to support her back when sitting and travelling. It proved most helpful for long trips, and we carried it like a suitcase.

When we expressed concern about irregular uterine bleeding, the gynecologist prescribed a hormonal treatment. Again, Bernice was apprehensive. "What will it do to me?" she asked. She read somewhere that pregnancy often cures this condition. "Can't wait for that," so we opted for a more feasible remedy—Vitamins E and B, plus a good supply of "personals."

A more pressing question seized her mind: "What shall I do when I graduate?" We visited Handicapped Manpower for assessment interviews. We had previously tried a similar computerized appraisal in Prince Albert. Their suggestion? Be a ship's purser. Wow! We must have missed the boat somewhere. But with the Manpower assessment, we had greater hopes because Bernice's knowledge of English and her aptitude for writing came to the fore. It was evident that computer skills would be essential for any job, so we determined to look into that possibility.

We went home fortified with Manpower's helpful suggestions, and greatly encouraged by Dr. Gerrard's comment that we were "managing the situation beautifully." He observed that "Bernice is remarkably well-adjusted to her handicap."

The Birch Hills Kinsmen Foundation kindly added Bernice's name to their list of those who would benefit from Telemiracle Funds. A computer would add speed and accuracy to her typing, and in anticipation of better things to come, she enrolled in a basic computer and business skills course in Prince Albert. I already felt inadequate at helping with her school work, and this only widened the gap. The instructor suggested I take the course with her. I didn't do it.

The unrelenting demands of learning and living left little time for social activity. We appreciated any distraction which focused our attention elsewhere. Two particularly significant weddings brought a welcome diversion.

On Bernice's birthday in 1978, Uncle Art Sundbo married Aunt Anna Boyes in Kenya. Though unable to attend, we celebrated with them in absentia.

The following year in August, Brian and Angie were married, still in their teens, young and full of hope. Bernice sat at the guest register. In time, three beautiful children were born to them, a delightful diversion which continues to this day.

Fall, 1979

In a routine checkup, Tom was diagnosed with prostate cancer. Suddenly, our mortality stared us in the face. Our happy, hard-working lifestyle would have to change. We sold the cattle, a wrenching decision. Those white-faced Herefords were family! Tom embarked on a series of radiation treatments at the Cancer Clinic in

Saskatoon. Thankfully, he recovered and was able to continue farming for several years.

Enter "The Seekers"

The demands of school work were not enough to focus Bernice's attention without wandering. Besides, Louise came only twice a week. Kneeling by the bed day after day with one's face in a book is dull and soul-deadening. Bernice confessed to spells of boredom and loneliness.

"I'd lie on the sofa, staring at the telephone, or I'd stand in the middle of the kitchen floor, looking longingly down the driveway, wishing someone would acknowledge my existence. Days, even weeks might go by without a personal phone call. Everybody was busy except me. I tried not to entertain a 'Why me, Lord?' attitude.

"One memorable afternoon, the phone rang. It was our neighbour, Alice Grambo, inviting me to Bible study at her home that evening. I didn't leap at the chance to go out because the prospect of meeting new people daunted me. But I went, thanks to Mom. Next week, same time, Alice phoned again. A small voice in my heart jolted me, 'Smarten up. You asked God to help you make friends. He is answering your prayer, so move!'

"I enjoyed the evening. Several in the group played instruments. We joined in the singing. A few weeks earlier I had purchased a tambourine. As we were about to leave that evening, Mom asked if they needed a tambourine player. They said sure, and so began a ministry that changed my life.

"The group began some months before to pray for definite community needs and to provide opportunity for

Bible study. Three couples formed the original nucleus, now grown to more than eighteen, aged sixteen to sixty, representing six denominations, divergent in some ways, but focused on a common goal.

"They had been asked to sing in several churches. We needed a name, other than 'group' or 'you guys'! We chose 'The Seekers,' based on Matthew 6:33: 'Seek ye first the kingdom of God, and His righteousness; and all these (other) things shall be added unto you.' Suddenly, I had friends who cared about me, and I had a way to share my faith. Singing came easier than speaking. It was a learning and growing process.

"Over three and a half years, we shared in 100 or more services. We travelled in a refurbished school bus with instruments and sometimes children in the back. Often the program was arranged en route and diligently practiced, only to have Clifford, our director, change the format as we stood on the platform. It kept us on our toes. Later, over coffee and goodies, we chatted with the local folks and were humbly gratified to hear that in spite of our unprofessional presentation, many were blessed. Little is much when God is in it.

"These tours covered many miles in northern Saskatchewan and Alberta, taking us to churches, halls, hospitals, nursing homes, fairgrounds and campgrounds. In November, 1982, a new opportunity presented itself. Someone asked if we would consider going to the Prince Albert Penitentiary Farm Annex. The suggested agenda was for an hour of singing and sharing Scriptures, followed by an hour of refreshments and socializing with the inmates. We had to be screened for entry, even though the annex is a minimum security facility.

"Was I ever nervous that day! All went well, despite our inward trembling. That first visit led to monthly appointments, a highlight for us and the inmates. A few of them occasionally shared their musical talents with us, resulting in a jam session.

"We encouraged them in their determination to wait patiently for the day of release. 'Commit thy way unto the Lord; trust also in Him,; and He shall bring it to pass' (Ps. 37:5). We kept in touch with one young man who later became a youth pastor. Others, who saw no light at the end of the tunnel, confided their problems and heartaches, a little at a time. Still others, close-mouthed and laconic, were reluctant to bare their souls before strangers.

"After many visits, we felt like friends. Occasionally, on a pass, an inmate spent a weekend in someone's home. We glimpsed, just a little, what it's like to be locked up, deprived of freedom and choice. The laws of man are based on the laws of God. Our Creator knows mutual respect for one another is the rule for peaceful co-existence. Rights and responsibilities go together. The Ten Commandments still apply. God is watching us from a distance.

"Our trips continued to be interspersed with my studies and exams, a happy arrangement for me. I was the only single in the group, and much younger, yet they accepted me as part of the family. I grew and blossomed in their fellowship."

Graduation, 1982

Mr. Boychuk, the principal, choreographed a memorable graduation for the six students who had arrived at this milestone. It was particularly gratifying for Bernice, for the tortoise had reached the finish line. She graduated with honours and delivered the valedictory address with a firm voice and trembling hands. I resisted the urge to help her be seated on the platform. Cousin Wes performed as her escort; Brian and his wife, Angie, came to share in her triumph.

"I couldn't believe it. Despite all odds, despite a physical handicap and many other hurdles in the race of life, I reached a milestone. I was graduating from high school. It was an incredible feeling to sit on stage with my classmates (even though I'd taken the last six years at home by correspondence). I gave the valedictory address with wobbly knees, tearful eyes and deep gratitude."

"Today we have reached the goal that seemed so far away when we started in grade one twelve years ago. There are many memories, most of them happy ones. These years have taught us many of the things we must know to live in today's world. Graduation signifies the door that is opening to us; the door to opportunity and hopefully, success.

"True success is not marked by money or possessions as much as how we act or react to circumstances around us. If we try our best at whatever vocation we choose and go at it wholeheartedly, we can succeed.

"The saying, 'It matters not whether you win or lose, but how you play the game' applies to the game of life as much as any other. If we follow the guidelines and exhortations set down for us by our parents and mentors, and profit from lessons learned by ourselves and others, we will have played the game well. These guidelines are not meant to be a burden but are given for our benefit.

"Our childhood and teenage years have been important in molding our future. We should think of our school years, not as drudgery, but as an instrument through which we learn to live with others and ourselves. Many people have contributed to our education during these years. The obvious ones are, of course, our parents and teachers. But we tend to forget that friends, neighbours and relatives also had a surprisingly great effect on us. We are grateful to all these people for helping us become the young adults we are today.

"I would like to thank the people who have been of special help to me. Without their support, I wouldn't be on this stage tonight. I thank the graduating class for including me in their graduation even though I am not a regular student here, and for giving me the honour of being valedictorian as well.

"I also thank God for giving me the strength and ability to carry on when I felt like giving up.

"Graduation marks the start of a new chapter in the book of our lives. It is not the end of learning, but the beginning. The story is told of a young college student who proclaimed boastfully to the world, 'I have graduated! I have my B.A.!' The world replied, 'Come with me and I'll teach you the rest of the alphabet.' Knowledge is the acquisition of facts. This is what we've been doing for the past twelve years. Wisdom, however, is the right use of these facts. This can be gained only by experience.

"In this time of unrest and uncertainty, we as young adults don't really know what our future will be like, or indeed, if there will be any future for us at all. But we must keep striving to make our mark in life by leaving the world a better place than when we arrived. Let us not follow where the beaten path may lead, but go instead where there is no path and make a trail for others to follow.

"In keeping with our graduation theme of 'Time,' I'd like to quote the chorus from a song: 'We have this moment to hold in *our hands and to touch as it slips through our fingers like sand, yesterday's gone and tomorrow may never come, but we have this moment today.'*

"As we make our plans, let us keep in mind the exhortation from the Bible found in Matthew 6:33: 'But seek first His Kingdom and His righteousness, and all these other things will be given you as well.' This is the secret of true success. Thank you and God bless you all."

CHAPTER FOUR

After Graduation

The party is over; the countdown has begun. Exams—one more hurdle. Bernice permitted herself only fleeting thoughts of what lay beyond. Then it was over. She rejoiced at her A+ standing, but wondered what to do with it. We missed Louise's weekly visits. No more deadlines, no more challenges.

Most students experience a letdown when school is over. Some, of course, have definite plans and find the transition easy. Bernice suffered a period of despondency. All her super-charged energy and will power had to be redirected. All suggestions were considered.

Bernice heard of a Bible College in the States. Sounds great, she said. In spite of our misgivings (or maybe because of), she contacted them. Bottom line: She would have to find her own accommodation and a caregiver to live with her. Discard that idea. An alternate suggestion came to mind.

"You have a good typewriter. Why not sign up for a course in Christian writing? You're good at that, so get started on a writing career."

She resurrected a few choice pieces from her English class and soon the typewriter was beating out a slow but steady rhythm in her room. She couldn't sit too long on the corner of the chair, so we had frequent snack breaks or music breaks. The electric organ with automatic rhythm provided a one-finger diversion at recess time.

Summer, 1982

"I was excited. For the first time in my life I was going to spend a week away from home, away from my parents and other older generation worry-warts. Mom was in Norway for two weeks and Dad would be staying on the farm. I was going to Saskatoon, eighty miles away, to stay with Tom and Brenda. Everything went great for the first three days or so. I was having a ball! Then on Wednesday, Brenda and I went to McDonald's for lunch. We were tooting down the stairs at a pretty good clip when all of a sudden the floor came up to meet me. Before I knew it, I was kissing the tile floor. After getting my bearings, I realized I had missed the bottom step, and because of my poor balance and fancy dress shoes, I came tumblin' down. So instead of getting our Big Mac, we had to head for the hospital to put five stitches on a cut above my left eyebrow. I was a mess. I had blood in my hair and on my new pink pants. Why me? My first time away from home... a great holiday... blown. To make matters worse, Mom had given strict orders before she left (she *always* gives strict orders!) to watch any steps I go on, and to always have someone helping me... neither of which I did. And when I fall, I fall... no holds barred, because I can't protect myself. Why me, Lord? Why now, Lord? Inside, I heard His answer and knew He was right. "You were careless. It was your fault... not Mine." But He was kind. Through the whole thing, it didn't hurt a bit. You'd think an incident as ugly as that would hurt at least a *little*. It felt tight from the swelling and I couldn't see much past the swollen eyelid. But even in my stupidity, God watched over me. It could have been *so* much worse. The need for surrender to His will and plan was being impressed on me during this time and I was balking it. This was God's way of making me realize my need of full dependency on Him. I was having such a good time on my own that I had forgotten to 'lean not on my own understanding' (Prov. 3:5-6).

"Through each seemingly negative situation, God draws me closer to Himself as I learn the hard way to praise Him even when the going is tough.

"I went to a bridal shower a few days after the fall and joked that I wore my outfit in different shades of purple to match my eye! Really giving thanks in all situations isn't easy, but it's worth it!"

This is My Life Today—Christmas Letter, 1982

"Maybe you would like to know what Bernice Boyes is doing now. Here goes!

"I'm taking a Christian journalism course by correspondence from the States. I finished a high school level accounting course and am now starting a business records course.

"I'm still going with The Seekers to Bible studies every Tuesday night and to places like the nursing home, churches and penitentiary.

"My parents and I still live on the farm, but I'm working on the possibility of moving to a larger center. I've learned to rest easy and allow God to lead. I've run ahead of Him and gone smack into problems too many times. Patience, Bernice, patience!

"My brother and sister-in-law live in Saskatoon and their son, Justin, is two. I couldn't ask for a better family. We're not perfect, but God put us together, and I'm glad He did! I love you all very much."

The Greatest Test

Help me to walk so close to Thee
That those who know me best can see
I live as godly as I pray.
And Christ is real from day to day.
I see some once a day, or year,
To them I blameless might appear;
'Tis easy to be kind and sweet
To people whom we seldom meet;
But in my home are those who see
Too many times the worst of me.
My hymns of praise were best unsung
If He does not control my tongue
When I am vexed and sorely tried
And my impatience cannot hide.
May no one stumble over me
Because Thy love they failed to see;
But give, my Lord, a life that sings
And victory over little things.
Give me Thy calm for every fear,
Thy peace for every falling tear;
Make mine, O Lord, through calm and strife

A gracious and unselfish life:
Help me with those who know me best
For Jesus' sake, to stand the test.

—Barbara C. Ryberg

Clouds on the Horizon

From Bernice's journal:

"The day of my birthday, April 15, 1983, dawned bright and clear. It was going to be such a special day—and it was. Many friends and relatives came over for coffee and cake in the afternoon. I was having a great time. I even got a call from one of my special sisters in Christ, Ruth, from my Bible study group. She was so happy and I was thrilled that she called.

"That night, we attended a special meeting. I was feeling fantastic! The next day, The Seekers were going to hold a service in a small town named Hendon. I was really looking forward to that. I woke up several times during the night in anticipation of the next day. At about 7:00 a.m., the phone rang. I decided it was one of Dad's sisters... they sometimes call early. I didn't bother to get up. The phone rang again at 7:30 and I was getting curious. I had an uneasy feeling. A few minutes later, Mom came into my room. 'Ruth Johnson had a brain hemorrhage. Clifford asked if you could phone Hendon and cancel.' My world crashed around me. Not Ruth! She just phoned yesterday to wish me a happy birthday. She was so happy. Just over two hours later, she collapsed.

"The whole morning was a blur. Phone calls, tears of unbelief. Anguish. She was on a respirator and someone called to tell us to come right away if we wanted to see her. We rushed to Prince Albert. I felt so weak, so helpless, so numb. I couldn't think straight for hours. We spent much of our time in the hospital's beautiful chapel, singing and praying. God was so close and we felt so close to each other."

Profoundly shaken by Ruth's death, Bernice struggled to make sense of God's dealings with His people.

"How can we get along without her? Don't You need her anymore, Lord? What about her children? You are aware of this, Lord. You surely have a plan. Some day we'll understand. After much agonizing I accepted God's sovereign will, in Ruth's case and in my own, and recommitted my life to Him, to go on by faith.

"More trials lay ahead. We lost two more from our group. Arvid suffered a massive heart attack, and Margaret died of cancer. Losing three members in the prime of life was very unsettling. With wounded hearts and diminished energy we continued. Duets and solos must be rearranged. It was painful. We comforted ourselves with our memories and the hope of eternal life. That was the message we still wanted to share."

Bernice kept a log of The Seekers' appointments and activities. She edited and typed their songbook, a collection of favourite country gospel songs and hymns, dedicated to Ruth.

The Woman Inside

In her junior years, Bernice didn't express much interest in boys as "boyfriends." Living with adults most of the time probably accounts for the fact that she was quite mature for her age... in outlook, not appearance.

Later, when she "fell" for someone, it was a much older man, and often a married man. Her infatuations had nothing to do with reality; it was her heart's flight of fancy. Once she was impressed with a doctor in Wakaw. She must have shared her feelings with her friends, as witness this entry in her autograph book:

> *If John Rempel lived across the sea*
> *What a good swimmer Bernice would be.*

An incident developed once when we attended special services in Prince Albert. She fell again, this time for the tenor soloist. Her insistence that we attend every service led to a heated discussion. We arrived at a compromise and concluded that our Bernice had a strong will, a useful attribute for persons with disabilities.

Bernice gradually accepted that she would never be married. She could cope with that, but envied girls who had boyfriends and dates. "I think the boys are afraid of me," she confided wistfully. "Maybe they don't know what to say to me, or they think I'll misunderstand their attention. I just wish someone would ask me out for coffee or something, so I could feel normal."

I hurt for her. *Come on, you guys, can't you see that my daughter is a fascinating person, taught of the Lord, and full of wisdom?* She had many "couple friends" who were a delight to her, who shared their love, their time, their hospitality and fellowship.

Her hope flared briefly again when she heard that Joni Eareckson had married. "Maybe there's a chance for me yet. I would need a man strong enough to carry me and the wheelchair. Oh, well, whatever You say, Lord."

"But my God shall supply all your need according to His riches in glory by Christ Jesus" (Phil. 4:19). She penned a tribute to the day she accepted that promise.

The Day I Found 'The' Man
by Bernice Boyes

I never thought it was fair that I had to be different. Every other young woman had someone to go out with, and I didn't. So I moped.

Until one day, one beautiful day, I encountered The Man. I can't say I was exactly swept off my feet—he isn't that type of friend. No, I'd say it was a gradual realization that he was the one God ordained for my life. Friend with a capital "F." He was no ordinary fellow. He understood so much and cared so much. He seemed to know more about the inner me than I knew myself. When I retreated into a shell, he coaxed me into the fresh air again. I called my problem inferiority complex; he called it pride. No beating around the bush for him!

When I felt hemmed in, he reminded me that I could be as free as I wanted to be. "But you don't understand. I have a physical handicap!" He understood. He'd also been through hard times.

My knight in glowing armor came to my rescue time after time. He glowed because he knew God in a unique way. If I could only feel a fraction of the closeness he felt to the Father, I'd be euphoric.

But there was always something standing between me and my friend, between me and the Father he loved so much. What was it? Suddenly it hit me.

I was always looking for more, when all I needed was within me. Greener pastures constantly beckoned, but the fence was always too high. I was frustrated. Discontented. I looked at other more "successful" people with envy. I watched couples exchanging wedding bands and longed for that intimacy.

One day he finally got tired of being subtle in getting through to me.

He turned my face toward his (so seldom do I really look him directly in the face), and he spoke to my spirit. What soothing words. What healing love flowed through my troubled heart as it dawned on me like the most beautiful sunrise imaginable. What he was saying was true! I don't need to wish for better things when I already have the best.

What did he say? He whispered so gently, "I am your Bridegroom. You are my Bride. I am all you need."

I cried. Oh yes, I see it now. He loved me so much that He would even be willing to die to give me the best life possible. That is love's supreme sacrifice.

And you know, He did. He did give His life. The hands that looked after my needs so well had nail scars.

■ ■ ■

In the fall of 1984, Tom's routine checkup revealed bone cancer. The reprieve was ending. Decisions had to be made.

"Maybe I could farm one more year," he said. "There's a lot of good summer fallow out there."

It didn't seem wise to add more stress to the body, engaged in its final battle for survival. We rented the land and sold the farm machinery. The following year we bought a house in Birch Hills and moved. These events can easily be related in brief statements, but each decision, with its ramifications, was an amputation, piece by piece, of a part of our lives.

Tom was born in that farm house. The soil was part of his psyche. He was a dedicated cattleman, a wise farmer, working in partnership with God. He would rather have stayed there to wait for God's call to come home, but he didn't want Bernice and me to be alone on the farm.

The auction sale was an experience to be borne with stoic fortitude. It helped a little that our old friend Bill Hodgins conducted the sale. We grieved a little, died a little, as each implement rolled out of the yard. The last farewell to a way of life. For Tom it meant the severing of so many fulfilling associations: the Co-op, the Credit Union, the Wheat Pool. We missed the close ties with good neighbours. Moving to Birch Hills meant leaving our friends at Wakaw Baptist Church. We found new friends and fellowship at Lake Park Baptist, but a part of us remained with the folk who had seen us through the mountain tops and valleys of our lives.

Tom grew weaker and experienced more pain. Eventually he was receiving morphine four times a day. He got dressed each morning but spent most of the time lying down or in the recliner. We read the Bible, talked, prayed and dozed together. He didn't want to go to the hospital. Thankfully, he was able to be at home most of the time. Bernice, who had moved to Saskatoon by then, came home. Brian and Angie and other family members spent time with us. In the afternoon of March 31, 1987, Tom left his body behind. In the presence of God, he now sees clearly the reality of what his faith had seen only "through a glass darkly."

We had humbly asked God for healing. Many had prayed likewise, anointing with oil in the name of Jesus. The healing we hoped for did not come, but we were thankful for eight years of reprieve.

Tom had faced death at other times in his life. During the war he was struck by a piece of shrapnel. A fellow soldier turned back and dragged him to safety. We remember with amazement the day he was caught in the leveling auger of the combine. His overalls and pant leg were ripped off but he walked to the house carrying the grain sample. God spared his life then, but not this time. There is an appointed time for our departure, and in the plan of God it is the right time. It didn't seem right to us then. Were it not for our conviction that this life is only a rehearsal for eternity with God, we would long ago have given in to discouragement.

His promise in Jeremiah 29:11 is long range. He sees one day as a thousand years and vice versa. He wants us to trust Him, for as Hebrews 11 says, "Without faith it is impossible to please Him."

"For I know the plans I have for you, declares the Lord, plans to prosper you and not to harm you, plans to give you hope and a future" (Jer. 29:11, NIV).

Moses reflected that three score and ten years is the average time allotted to our earthly journey. Some more, some less. The hope and a future God speaks of, from His eternal perspective, reaches far beyond the grave.

The infinity aspect of our destiny in no way lessens the significance of the here and now. The word He left behind for our guidance is rich with tender love. "I am the good shepherd, the good shepherd giveth His life for the sheep.... I know My sheep and am known of Mine.... I have loved thee with an everlasting love; therefore with loving-kindness have I drawn thee.... I am the bread of life; he that cometh to Me shall never hunger; and he that believeth in Me shall never thirst.... My grace is sufficient for thee; for My strength is made perfect in weakness.... I will ask the Father, and He will give you another counselor to be with you forever... the Spirit of truth.... I go to pre-pare a place for you.... I will come again to receive you unto Myself... because I live you shall live also" (John 10:11,14; Jer. 31:3; John 6:35; 2 Cor. 12:9; John 14:16).

As his grasp on life began to slip, Tom committed his family to God. He thanked God for a good life, and for the hope he would soon see his Saviour face to face.

We carry on, "looking for that blessed hope, and the glorious appearing of the great God and our Saviour Jesus Christ" (Titus 2:13).

CHAPTER FIVE

The Call of the Wild

August 5, 1984, from Bernice's journal

"**M**y mind has been a whirlpool of confusion these past few months. I just *knew* God was calling me to go somewhere... anywhere but where I was. Maybe He is, but not right away. He has other plans for me right here, right now. 'Be content with such things as you have,' He says. But I wasn't. I wanted to get out of my present circumstances. I wanted freedom. Paul, despite his many reverses, still declared, 'I have learned, in whatever state I am, therewith to be content.' Maybe contentment *is* freedom. If I'm irritable and dissatisfied here at home, a change of location wouldn't help. If I can learn by God's grace to become truly content right where He, in His perfect plan, has placed me, then I can know His peace. 'My peace I give unto you, not as the world giveth.... Let not your heart be troubled' (John 14:27).

"Forgive me, Lord, I was trying to *make* Your will happen, or mine perhaps, instead of *letting* You lead. That route leads to frustration. The oil of joy dries up. The wheels squeal instead of sing. I want to shine for You, Jesus. Help me to let Your love shine through me.

"So Lord, we'd better start right now; we've got a lot to do! 'The Lord will guide you continually' (Isa. 58:11, TLB).

"As far as God's will for my life is concerned, I'm discovering one very important thing. I've prayed for years, 'Lord, what is Your plan for my life?' I expected a lightning bolt answer that would sound something like this:

"'Well, Bernice, I want you to move to this city next week, into this apartment on this street and work in this office for five years and thirteen days. Then I want you to quit that job and move to this house in this city and buy a Christian bookstore. Then, on your thirty-fifth birthday, sell everything and go to Africa to start a revival among the pygmies.'

"That's not the way God works, is it? He doesn't hand out blueprints saying, 'This is your life.' God reveals His will one day at a time, one step at a time. The ultimate goal is to become more and more like Jesus and less and less like my old self. God will use various methods to help me work toward that goal. In His own way, in a still, small voice, God will show me what He wants me to do as I come to each crossroad. Sometimes God does use the supernatural or the spectacular to reveal His will, but that isn't an everyday experience for everybody. When God closes one door, He always prepares to open another.

"Often I've been so busy feeling sorry for myself, so wrapped up in my petty peeves that I can't see God's hand reaching down to guide me. Maybe He's leading me in a different direction than I had in mind. I have discovered He never forces Himself on me. If I refuse to take the path He is trying to show me, He will patiently wait until I've turned back to His way. Often I have to stumble over my selfish nature and slip in the muck. Sometimes I lie there for a while, too lazy to get up, not allowing Him to lift me. When I try to get back on my feet, however, I just slide around. The longer I struggle, the worse it becomes. I finally give up and cry, 'Help, Lord!' I'm covered with mud from head to foot but Jesus gives me a big bear hug anyway and washes me clean. What refreshment. What joy. What peace.

"At those times, I'm reminded that I must learn 'to put aside [my] own desires so that I will become patient and godly, gladly letting God have His way with [me]' (2 Peter 1:6, TLB).

"It's neat to know when I surrender like that, His will *becomes* my will. I want to do what He has for me to do. I won't have real peace any other way.

"An example: I desperately wanted to go to a Bible college in the States last year. I bulldozed my way into applying (against most people's discretion... what do they know anyway?) and was well on my way to being accepted. But obstacles came up. My handicap posed a big problem since I needed a roommate to help me. And I didn't know anyone who could do this. I stubbornly hung on and sent in my forms. It sounded so exciting to go off to a distant college, away from everyone I know. Wow, what was I thinking?

"The final blow was a letter from the college explaining I would have to find my own accommodation as they had no way of helping me in that area. That was it. I couldn't do anything about it. I was discouraged for a while, but now I know I was running ahead of God. 'Stay home, Bernice. I have something else in mind that's far more exciting than what you planned.'

"*Seek* and you shall find, *ask* and it shall be given, *knock* and the door will be opened unto you, says Matthew 7. I was pulling on the doorknob instead of knocking!"

> *Have Thine own way, Lord,*
> *Have Thine own way.*
> *Thou art the Potter,*
> *I am the clay.*
> *Mold me and make me*
> *After Thy will,*
> *While I am waiting*
> *Yielded and still.*

—A.A. Pollard

Bernice heard that the "God Uses Ink" Christian writers' seminar would be offered at Canadian Bible College in Regina.

"Wow! Just what I need to pep me up and give me some new ideas!"

One of the instructors that year was Brian Stiller, then-president of the Evangelical Fellowship of Canada. Certainly, Bernice gleaned valuable information on communicating thoughts, but meeting Brian Stiller proved to be the seminar's most lasting benefit. As they kept in touch over the years, he shared his biblical world view and his concern for the moral and spiritual decline of our nation.

Bernice prayed for him and his colleagues as they sought to combat this drift away from God. He convinced her that dedicated prayer support for those in public ministry is vital to them and the outcome of their work. From that time Bernice offered herself to the Lord as a prayer helper. She kept a file of correspondents from many parts of the world, who shared their needs and victories with her.

"I can pray anytime," she exclaimed excitedly. "In bed, waiting to go to bed, having my hair done, in the bathroom. The line to God is always open. I can write when the time is right, but I can pray anytime. Thank You, heavenly Father, for listening."

Bernice wrote a story about a young eagle perched on the edge of the nest, contemplating the vastness around him, trying to muster the courage to take off. He extends his wings, sways on his perch, then folds his wings and slumps down. It takes concentration. Bernice saw herself in this story. While mother eagle may have given her youngster a strategically planned push, Bernice's mom was tugging on the coattails.

Clearly, our bird wanted to fly. With the hurdle of moving from the farm finally over and Tom's health still reasonably stable, we decided to look for a suitable care home in Saskatoon. We visited several facilities, comfortable enough, but not appropriate for Bernice. She needed space and youth and mobility. As we left one place, she said, "Over my dead body!"

"Hey, Bernice! Maybe home doesn't look so humdrum after all!"

Finally, we were directed to John and Martha Janzen. They had a spacious new home, four young residents, and an extended family who visited often. Bernice could attend Westgate Alliance Church with them. Ideal. We praised the Lord for His guidance. In September, 1986, Bernice moved into her cozy room.

She spent long periods at the typewriter, perched on the corner of her chair, the stiff left leg hanging down. Though her arms were fixed in front of her chest (flexion contractions they called it), her typing speed was quite acceptable. The long-awaited computer arrived, adding inspiration and enthusiasm to her efforts. Her dream of a "this is my life" story had begun to take shape over the past year or two, much of it labouriously handwritten. Cousin Ellen Johnston typed it for her in a more professional format. She added to it as life went on.

City life offered new and rich experiences. She made many friends at church. One was Cheryl, who had recently lost her sight in an automobile accident. They became soul mates, sharing their faith and their disabilities. The National Institute for the Blind provided a seeing eye dog for Cheryl, as well as training sessions to help her adjust to the dog and overcome her fear of going out, riding buses and making mistakes without embarrassment.

Learning to live a normal life in the dark was a struggle. Bernice became her encourager. In their symbiotic relationship, Bernice's eyes served them both; Cheryl provided reach and strength when needed. They played miniature golf, went shopping and sightseeing. They ate out and ate at Cheryl's apartment. Cooking was sometimes a challenge. When Bernice dropped some chicken on the floor, Cheryl picked it up as Bernice gave instructions as to its whereabouts. The dog, well-trained and obedient, was able to restrain himself from involvement in the action.

Bernice's fertile mind sought opportunities and activities where she could be helpful. She joined a singles group, open to people of all ages and situations. Her horizons expanded. The Western Tract Mission needed volunteers. This developed into a part-time job as she became involved in the Children's Mail Box Club.

In May, shortly after Tom's death, Martha Janzen had to give up her residents due to ill health. We were sorry for her and sorry to leave. We prayed for one another. Bernice's bulky possessions were stored at Brian's place, and she came home with me to Birch Hills. The search resumed for another care home.

Meanwhile, Aunt Dorothy had retired and moved to Birch Hills. Not only that, she was engaged to be married in August to John Gray, an old friend. To occupy the intervening weeks, she taught Vacation Bible School in Prince Albert. Bernice went as her helper. Preparations for the wedding kept us busy and excited all summer. Tom was to have given the bride away, but instead, he watched from heaven. Brother Stanley came from British Columbia to escort Dorothy down the aisle. Brian and family, with many relatives and friends, shared this happy event. The two missionary aunties, who had set aside their teaching careers and hopes of family life in order to help others, were now blessed with exemplary Christian husbands. Praise God, the creator and sustainer of the universe, who also is aware of us, individuals made in His image, on our sojourn here on planet earth.

Shortly after the wedding, we investigated a prospective care home for Bernice in Saskatoon. Heather and Doug, with their young son and daughter, operated a care home for seniors, but agreed to consider Bernice. With her room in the basement, I was concerned about the few steps to be navigated several times a day. Bernice, however, saw this as no great problem. The room was comfortable, with large windows, so we signed on the dotted line.

The move this time proceeded more easily. Before long the computer was hooked up and humming, and in short order, Bernice had re-established links with the church, Western Tract Mission, Cheryl and others.

"This will be just fine, Mom. Don't worry about the stairs at all. I'll be careful. Love you, Mom. Thanks for everything."

I went home, but my heart stayed. I often used my hot line to God.

Bernice lived in the family residence with Doug, the children and another boarder. Heather lived at a nearby residence with several seniors so they alternated in the performance of their duties. The following year, as space became available, Bernice moved to the second residence. There again she had a basement room, but larger. She had fun arranging her furniture to create the illusion of office at one end and bedroom at the other. She added decorative touches to blend with her new comforter. She was ecstatic with the results.

Doug's family soon became friends as well as care-givers. The care was excellent, and as friends they encouraged her in her social contacts and new endeavours. She and Doug had many stimulating discussions over lunch, probing the meaning of life, the hope of life everlasting and how one may find it.

Bernice determined to get acquainted with the senior residents and be a friend to them. She knew from experience that a disability can set you apart from the mainstream of life. Seniors, afflicted with hearing loss, poor eyesight and failing memory, are more so at risk of being ignored. Life can become a tedious daily routine of waiting to die. One dear lady, frail and clinging to life, her dark eyes searching for a response when someone passed her, whispered, "Talk to me, I'm in here."

Responding to such fundamental human need takes time and patience, rare commodities in our hurried lifestyle. We have, of course, all the time there is, but the priorities as to its use are set somewhere in the back room of the mind. Peter Ustinov expressed it pointedly: "Charity is more common than compassion because charity is tax deductible, while compassion is merely time consuming."

Bernice determined to give her time, empathy and love to cheer the seniors' daily lives. She adopted Edna Banting, the widow of a Baptist minister, for regular morning visits, to read to her and pray. Our hearts ached for one gentleman, stricken with Alzheimer's. Formerly a successful accountant, he couldn't remember how to dress himself. May God shed light into the inner recesses of the mind, the seat of the spirit, where the Creator can detour around the short circuits and communicate spirit to spirit.

For a while the computer was lonely, humming to itself downstairs. The files were organized all right: lists of prospective publishers, query letters to send, ideas to explore, articles sent, articles returned, all in order. Occasionally Bernice filed an article or poem under "accepted." Hallelujah! Needed now, though, were motivation, enthusiasm and brilliant ideas. Yet, any distraction—a phone call or invitation out for coffee—was eagerly accepted. The computer screen glared accusingly.

"'Writing is so much more than putting pen to paper and forming a chain of words. Sometimes it's communicating facts or feelings. Sometimes it's talking from the heart. Or off the top of your head. It can mean a lot to the writer and the reader. Or it can mean little. You can write because you want to or because you have deadlines. It can be a hobby, a part-time occupation or a full-time job. But always it is communicating part of yourself, your thoughts and ideas. It's a powerful way to touch the world. I feel honoured that God has allowed me to be part of it.'

"The foregoing is a quote from my writing course assignment. Sounds cool and masterful. Now, it seems, I've lost my unction (temporarily, of course). I'm baffled. I don't know what to write. Please help me to think of something to say. What should a Christian writer write about? Have I run out of steam? Have I missed the boat somewhere? Should I take a course? Go to school again? I have been back-pedaling lately. I'm sorry, Lord, for neglecting the gift You gave me. I want to be a witness for You in this world. I've allowed things to distract me. I admit it."

Self-centeredness
laziness
time wasting
T.V.
shopping
wanting attention
wanting limelight
wanting a boyfriend
wanting sympathy
moping
neglect of Your Word
neglect of prayer
neglect of fellowship with You

> *being insensitive*
> *going to extremes one way or another*
> *crawling into my shell.*

"There You have it, Lord. It's all on the table. Forgive me. Holy Spirit, shine in my heart with a new inspiration. Let my motivation come from You. 'Being confident of this very thing, that He which hath begun a good work in you will perform it' (Phil. 1:6). Thank You, Lord."

October, 1987

"Dear friends:

"'For I know the plans I have for you, declares the Lord, plans to prosper you and not to harm you, plans to give you hope and a future' (Jer. 29:11, NIV).

"He 'knows the plans.' As I look at how my life has changed over the past two years, I really understand what that verse is saying. I not only have a future, I have a HOPE. And each detail has significance.

"When I moved to the city, I volunteered two days a week at Western Tract Mission... with The Mailbox Club (Bible correspondence) Department. I advanced from helping to correct and grade lessons for instructors, to processing a course on my own.

"My job description: File student grades and letters, prepare new lessons for mailing, plan an occasional flyer, search for and enclose tracts and booklets that might be of particular interest or help to students, and most challenging of all, answer student letters and questions to establish a friendship.

"Many kids don't have anyone to talk to when they have a problem or need encouragement. It thrills me to be their confidante. A good number of students are not Christians (yet!). Some come from families where there is little godly encouragement. Even those from Christian homes sometimes need an outsider to share with.

"My ultimate dream (that's biblical, right?) is to start a Christian support group for needs-oriented individuals in the city, using some ideas from Joni Eareckson Tada's ministry. Right now, I'm praying about starting a phone ministry to the elderly, those who are lonely and would love to receive a phone call once a day, or whatever.

"I will be sending out a prayer letter quarterly. If you would like to receive it, please let me know.

"May the joy of Jesus shine on your day. He is ABLE!"

Because He Lives!
Bernice Boyes

March, 1988

"Dear friends:

"'I am only one but I am still one. I cannot do everything, but I can still do something.'

"The past few months have been exciting! On December 15, I received my first cheque as a part-time staff member at Western Tract Mission. Actually, it was my first paycheque EVER! And you, my friends and supporters, have made it possible.

"The real reason why I'm thrilled is that I can combine ministry with making my "bread." I can work with my students, something I love, and be meeting my financial needs as well.

"Talk about having my cake and eating it, too!

"You wouldn't believe the number of letters I receive from hurting kids (and some adults, as well). Many notes that come to us are simply friendly greetings, 'I have three brothers and a pet rabbit, Alex.' But as I earn their respect and friendship, they begin to be honest about their struggles, and I often cry to the Lord for wisdom and grace to be what they really need.

"Western Tract Mission underwent some renovations recently so a lot of changes are occurring structurally. But the spirit of the work is the same, and we go on (through the dust!) with joy in serving Jesus. As the office settles back into a routine, I look forward to new open doors for my ministry at WTM. I am working to expand what I am doing for my students, and possibly helping to alleviate some of my supervisor's heavy workload. I'll fill you in on that next time.

"I must close for now. I am expecting Cheryl this evening. She is also an answer to prayer as she and I can understand each other so well. She may be physically blind, but together we can 'see' so much! We went miniature golfing on Saturday. I lined her up and she putted. What fun!"

Joyfully yours, Bernice

August 23, 1988—Saskatoon, SK

"Dear friends:

"*A woodpecker was pecking on a great tree. Suddenly, a huge bolt of lightning struck the tree and, with enormous noise and force, split it down the middle, to its roots. The poor little woodpecker found himself on the ground nearby, half-dead, his feathers torn and singed. And when he gathered himself together he croaked, 'I didn't know I could do it!'*

"God's power makes the biggest lightning bolt look like a dim night light, and I have no more strength to split a redwood tree than a woodpecker, yet God chooses to work through me.

"At the Mailbox Club, work continues to expand... we received more responses over the past few weeks. This could be partly due to a new project I have taken on. In early June, I printed up the first edition of a newsletter for the kids in our club. I asked for their input, their jokes, stories, poems, and favourite Bible verses. I received a fantastic response. The students love the idea... it gives them a chance to participate and get to know about other students as well. We've even included a pen pal column! I ran a contest to find a name for it and we came up with '*The Good News Express.*'

"I continue with my writing, recently spurred on by an afternoon visit with an author from the States, Margaret Jensen. She was the speaker at Mom's church a couple of weeks ago.

"Well, it's time for a coffee break, so I guess I'll go. Wish you could join me.

"Have a super-duper day. Because He lives, I LIVE. Not just existing, but LIVING!

Love 'n' prayers,
Bernice Boyes

"P.S. Remember, God can use a crooked stick to draw a straight line."

Excerpts from Bernice's journal that summer of '89 reveal some of her struggles and victories:

"'As the deer panteth for the water, so my soul longs for Thee... why art thou cast down, oh my soul? They that wait upon the Lord shall renew their strength' (Ps. 42:1,5; Isa. 40:31). Thank You, Lord.

"My future with Jesus is secure and exciting, It doesn't matter how long you live, but how well you live each day. For the Christian, that is even more important in this world of hopelessness and unrest. We can personally know the Author of true hope and perfect rest."

May 21, 1989

"Dear Jesus:

"It's been many days since I last wrote to You. Today, living with seniors has gotten to me. Two are in the hospital, one with a stroke, the other with colon cancer. Life for them is discouraging. Forgetful, deaf and blind, they're just existing, living from meal to meal, visit to visit (often far between).

"Lord, may I never allow my life to be humdrum and empty. I am young. They've lived their lives. I haven't. I need to LIVE! Show me, Father, how to be a spark plug in this home, to bring a little vitality to their lonely days, and not let their despondency affect me. Help me in this, Jesus, to be Your hand extended in Heather's care home.

"I am often reminded to pray for those in leadership in the Christian community. There's a battle between the forces of light and darkness. May we resist that darkness in Jesus' name. Lord, be our shield and protection. The gates of hell shall not prevail against Your church, provided we advance! Onward, Christian soldiers!

"As I go to sleep tonight, Lord, wrap me in the blanket of Your love. I need Your wisdom, Your warmth of Spirit to be all You meant me to be on earth.

"Guide me as to Your plans for me in the future. Really start opening doors, Lord. *Show* me. Teach me patience (a dangerous thing to ask, I realize, but I need it!). Sensitivity and boldness too, Lord. Opposites sometimes, but both are needed."

May 23, 1989

"I had an interesting talk with Doreen last night. It seems we are a lot alike in our spiritual pilgrimage. We both seek a Spirit-led life, and feel a dearth of teaching on the Holy Spirit. We need a touch from You, Sweet Spirit. Restore Your Church again!"

Father, we worship You so superficially.
We treat You like the "Guy upstairs"
Or like a Vegas slot machine.
If we work at You long enough, we can get
exactly what we want. We can hit the jackpot.
You cry out, "Come unto Me," but we are too busy...
Too busy doing our own thing to bother to listen.
You ask us to give the "sacrifice of praise"
but we can't be bothered.
Or we think, "Hey, I don't have to sacrifice anything
because I'm a child of the King!"
Oh, how it must grieve You when Your own people refuse
to take up their crosses and follow You.
We say, "That isn't what I signed up for,
Miracles, blessings, prosperity... that's where it's at."
I can hear Your voice crying in the wilderness
of Your Church today:
"Whom shall I send and who will go for us?"
Silence.
Satan has put tranquilizers in the wine of the Church.
Your Church, Lord. My Church.
Don't leave us, oh God. Wake us up. Revive us...

Before it is too late. Forgive us. Restore us.
Lord...?

—Bernice Boyes

June 10, 1989

"Dear Jesus:

"Yes, I know it's been awhile. No excuse. A lot has happened. I've been asked to appear on 100 Huntley Street. I would like to use this letter to prepare my heart and soul for September 8.

"What do you want me to say, Jesus? Ester says I should tell them I walk a fine line health-wise all the time. So many things *could* go wrong, yet my times are in Your hands. I'll *live* as long as I live. I'll work to do my best with what I've got. And in turn, You, Lord, keep me free from pain with a disease that is supposed to be painful. Keep Your hand over me to shield me from Satan's arrows.

"I really *do* believe, Lord, that You are more than capable of healing me. And I *don't* want to in *any* way inhibit Your power from working in me or through me. Maybe I've become hardened by the dozens of times I've been prayed for. Soften me to Your Spirit's wooing, Jesus. Please speak to my heart so I may follow You. Not because of what others say, but because You are Lord. You have a plan.

"Give me renewed hunger for You, Jesus. A renewed thirst for Your Word. A renewed baptism of Your Holy Spirit with all the fire and zeal You desire to shower on me. Burn away the dross; all the wood, hay and stubble that I have stuffed in the cracks of Your sure foundation.

May the words I speak, and the meditation of my heart be acceptable in Your sight, O Lord, my Rock, my Strength, my Redeemer. May my *every* word, *every* thought, any *every* action be tempered by Your Spirit's wisdom, grace and power."

June 15, 1989

"Dear Jesus:

"Set me free from the spirit of fear regarding my health. Forgive me for worrying when I should be trusting. Help me be content to be single. You give me so many opportunities and friends who bless my life. I thank You for them.

"My eyes are on You, Lord. I give You my life. Take it, use it, glorify Yourself through it any way You please. It's Yours.

"Grant me courage, strength, purpose, hope, patience, joy, wisdom, direction, unction, the fullness of Your Spirit's power every day to be the person You want me to be. May I decrease, and may You increase. I love You, Jesus. Amen."

Bernice copied Chisholm's famous hymn into her diary.

Oh, To Be Like Thee

Oh, to be like Thee, blessed Redeemer
This is my constant longing and prayer
Gladly I'll forfeit all of earth's treasure
Jesus, Thy perfect likeness to wear.

Oh, to be like Thee, full of compassion
Loving, forgiving, tender and kind
Helping the helpless, cheering the fainting
Seeking the wandering sinner to find.

Oh, to be like Thee, lowly in spirit
Holy and harmless, patient and brave

Meekly enduring cruel reproaches
Willing to suffer, others to save.

Oh, to be like Thee, Lord, I am coming
Now to receive th' anointing divine
All that I am and have I am bringing
Lord, from this moment, all shall be Thine.

Oh, to be like Thee, while I am pleading
Pour out Thy Spirit, fill with Thy love
Make me a temple meet for Thy dwelling
Fit me for life and heaven above.

Oh, to be like Thee, Oh, to be like Thee
Blessed Redeemer, pure as Thou art
Come in Thy sweetness, come in Thy fullness
Stamp Thine own image deep on my heart.

—Thomas Chisholm

June 21, 1989

"Dear Jesus:

"Today Mom goes to Norway for a trip that is to be enjoyed, but also I believe it will have eternal ramifications. Go before her, Lord, prepare the way.

"Go before me too, Jesus, as I walk into this day. Keep me under the shadow of Your wings.

"A derivative of the word 'tribulation' is 'threshing.' As a farmer's daughter I know all about that. Help me to persevere, as chaff and straw are threshed out of my life. May only golden grain remain.

"Compassion, Christ's compassion. Not just patient or impatient tolerance with those in need, but full-fledged, selfless love and attention given wholeheartedly with no sense of getting any payback.

"Open doors for me, Jesus, and give me the grace and strength to walk through them. Keep me humble, as scary as that prayer may be!"

> *My eyes are on you, Lord,*
> *My eyes are on you.*
> *Heal me, restore me*
> *As I praise and adore thee,*
> *My eyes are on you, Lord,*
> *My eyes are on you.*
>
> —Author unknown

August 23, 1989

"Dear Jesus:

"It's been a long while, but today I want to copy a poem which means a lot to me. Let Your will become mine, Lord."

> *I asked God for strength*
> *that I might achieve;*
> *I was made weak*
> *to humbly obey.*
> *I asked for health*
> *that I might do greater things;*
> *I was given infirmity*
> *that I might do better things.*
>
> *I asked for riches*
> *that I might be happy;*
> *I was given poverty*
> *that I might be wise.*

I asked for power
that I might have the praise of men;
I was given weakness
that I might feel the need of God.
I asked for all things
that I might enjoy life;
I was given life
that I might enjoy all things.
I got nothing I asked for
But everything I had hoped for.
I am among all men
most richly blessed.

—Roy Campanella

"As the deer pants for water, so I long for you, O God. I thirst for God, the living God" (Ps. 42:1-2, TLB).

"My soul thirsteth for God. Why art thou cast down, oh my soul, and why art thou disquieted within me? Hope thou in God, for I shall yet praise Him for the help of His countenance" (Ps. 42:5).

September, 1989

In the rush of preparing to leave for Toronto, Bernice set her diary aside. Anticipation charged every waking minute with excitement. She loved travelling and remembered with pleasure other interesting family expeditions over the years: twice to Virginia to visit friends, she waded in the Atlantic shallows... once to Wisconsin to touch base with a co-worker and friend of mine from South Africa days... and many Canadian holidays in our little trailer, including several times to Vancouver to visit Aunt Alice. This Toronto trip, however, had special significance for we would meet David Mainse and staff, whose faces and voices had grown familiar to us on the 100 Huntley Street program.

Moira Brown, the charming hostess, put us at ease immediately. In the course of pre-interview, make-up and seating arrangement, Bernice met Bob Wieland, another guest. He had lost both legs in Vietnam. Having developed amazing arm strength, he could propel himself wherever he wanted to go. Bernice was impressed.

"My arms are pretty well zero," she admitted, "but I still have fairly reasonable legs. Thank You, Lord."

As show time drew near, we took our places, I in the visitors' gallery, Bernice on a precarious stool. She came through the interview like a pro, following her outline of significant points: my body is disabled, I'm not; a brief history of the disease; my spiritual history: how Jesus found me; challenge; what we do with what we have; my mission: writing and intercession; my vision: acceptance and opportunity for the disabled; God can use a crooked stick to draw a straight line (2 Cor. 4:7-10,16-18).

After lunch in the cafeteria we toured the building. We marveled at the technology, skill and planning necessary to produce a daily program we take for granted. Thank God for the vision He gave David Mainse to launch this ministry, a vision he has passed to thousands of supporters. We were challenged to "hold the ropes" in prayer and giving, so the message of salvation will continue to be heard.

As we waited in the vestibule for Uncle Dave to pick us up, Bernice glanced in a mirror. "Mom! We forgot to take off the make-up! I've been walking around all afternoon with make-up on!"

"Don't worry about it. You look quite elegant, dressed up and radiant. You always look radiant. Max Factor can't improve on it."

Uncle Dave took us to the SIM headquarters to spend some time with him and Aunt Shirley. They were hosts and caretakers of this complex mission agency which supervises hundreds of missionaries and provides hospitality to them as they move in and out of the Toronto area.

Another aunt and uncle, Sue and Les Elliott, arrived from Rosseau Lake, north of Toronto, to share their hospitality with us. We spent a few days at their cottage, cruising the lake and enjoying northern scenery.

En route to Toronto for our return flight, Bernice persuaded Uncle Les to take us to a mall. She just had to experience a big city mall, and experience it she did, for two hours. She didn't miss anything. I could hardly keep up with her. In retrospect, she seemed compelled to see it all, do it all, now. It was the last time she shopped on foot.

CHAPTER SIX

The Detour

In our travels we often come upon a road sign which advises us: Be Prepared to Stop, or Detour Ahead. Detours happen in life experiences too, sometimes without warning. The cautionary advice to be prepared then fortifies the inner man against unexpected and potentially traumatic experiences. Bernice encountered in 1989 what might be called a life-changing event, though she was not exactly a stranger to such happenings. She had learned over the years to be confident that He who had begun a good work in her would continue to perform His will and purpose in her life. He who sees the past, present and future as one large tapestry shapes our circumstances to conform to the master plan.

Late in September, 1989, Bernice noticed a taut feeling in her upper right leg. Flashbacks to similar discomforts caused some concern, but we decided to attend the Briercrest Bible College conference. Not a wise decision.

A tender, firm area about two inches in diameter had developed inside the upper thigh, obviously a new outbreak of her disease. We hastily prepared to leave, dreading the long trip ahead of us. We lifted Bernice into the bus and padded the seat with cushions. Three hours later we arrived in Saskatoon. Heather met us. We helped Bernice down the stairs to her room. A wordless knowing passed between us. I saw in Bernice's eyes the dawning of a new reality: "I'm losing the use of my good leg."

Relieved to be horizontal, Bernice retired to bed with Tylenol and tender, loving care. I slept on a mattress on the floor. By morning, the swelling had almost reached the knee, as Dr. Gerrard described it, "inexorable." Walking, or indeed moving at all, was very painful. She could stand for brief periods to eat. Often at night she would awaken, needing to be turned, use the bedpan or take a Tylenol. We used these intervals to have a little talk with Jesus. "He giveth His beloved sleep." We were thankful for peace, an answer to many prayers on our behalf. We felt supported and cushioned.

Three days later the entire leg was involved. We used her lace-up shoe to keep her foot at right angles. Distended and hard, the leg refused to obey instructions. When it was necessary to move from place to place, the leg had to be dragged. Doug, her caregiver, washed her hair over the edge of the tub as she lay horizontally across my lap and two chairs. We managed to get a few laughs out of that procedure.

We kept a journal of each day's progress or set back, thanking God for His presence and promises. We didn't know then that this would be a marathon of struggle and hope extending into weeks, then months. *One day at a time, sweet Jesus.*

Friends and family members came to cheer and console. Cheryl and her dog, her mother, Tena, and brother, Ken, arrived with Chinese food. Pastor Keith brought a converter for the TV. From her bed, surrounded by the TV remote, the phone and a tape player, Bernice was in charge of her environment. Pastor Keith and others from Westgate Alliance Church came to pray for her. *We trust You, Lord. You know the way through this wilderness.*

October 13. Bernice was transferred by ambulance to Royal University Hospital in Saskatoon. I stayed overnight with Brian's family. It was snowing. Uncle Art Sundbo shared a Scripture passage for Bernice as we talked on the phone: "I know, O Lord, that Thy judgments are right and that Thou in faithfulness hast afflicted me. Let, I pray Thee, Thy merciful kindness be for my comfort, according to Thy Word unto Thy servant" (Ps. 119:75-76).

Bernice reported such luxuries as a whirlpool bath and a Kinair bed. The latter, especially created for burn victims and very expensive, was temporarily made available to Bernice. Dr. Rudachyk, from the rehabilitation ward, came to assess Bernice. Visitors appeared everyday, providing cheer and diversion. Uncle Joe, Aunt Gladys, Lorelie and Wes shared much good humour. Doreen, Cheryl and Shawn were regulars. Brian and Angie called in en route from work. Doug could be counted on to show up every day, usually with some food.

October 18. Moved down to the rehabilitation ward. It was more informal there. Dr. Rudachyk explained a new treatment, Didronel, a drug which hopefully would prevent calcium from being laid down in the muscle. A bone scan may reveal to what extent this had already happened.

Bernice phoned Heather to relinquish her room. There were tears. She also considered resigning from the Mission. Hard decisions.

I stayed with Bernice every day and most nights. We made use of reclining chairs, love seats and the Quiet Room furniture. Occasionally, a respite bed was thankfully accepted at Brian's home, Gladys' second floor and the Ganes' home. Bernice went to physiotherapy for assessment: motion was very limited. The leg ached continually. They tried ice packs and an electrical device to relieve pain. The occupational therapy technician called in to review possibilities in that area. Bernice joked that the tongue was the only part of her anatomy that still moved freely.

October 23. I went home on the bus to replenish my suitcase wardrobe. Doreen shared a video with Bernice, and Cheryl stayed all afternoon. Doug moved Bernice's things to Doreen's place. Jan, her computer helper, disconnected the computer before moving. It was a relief, though tinged with sadness, to have this done. That room, Bernice's "pad" as she called it, held many happy memories.

October 25. Doug took Bernice for a ride in the wheelchair. Checked out the second floor gift shop. Pastor Keith and several from the singles group dropped in for a visit. Bernice had a poor night. Her leg was hard and unyielding. We noticed her stomach appeared bloated. I slept in the Quiet Room across the hall, about four hours. Tylenol at 3:30 brought some relief. Next morning after breakfast we heard someone's tape player down the hall: "Farther along we'll know all about it; farther along we'll understand why." We chuckled a little and added, "Amen, thank You for that assurance, Lord."

October 27. Dr. Rudachyk had a long talk about Bernice's condition. She said they wanted to keep Bernice on the medication another week and then check results. The swelling was moving up to the lower back and buttocks. Her back and side were sore and aching, maybe from lying in bed so long. Gladys brought a sheepskin which proved to be a great help.

October 29. Bernice threw up in the morning. This problem persisted all day so they restricted food and tried liquids. Angie stayed for a few hours to help. The vomiting continued. Next day they started IV and cut off everything by mouth. Dr. Miller and Dr. Litwin came to check Bernice's abdomen for appendix and other potential problems. Blood was tested, output measured and analyzed. There was a question as to the cause of this latest development. Bernice and I consulted the Great Physician as well. There were phone calls from Margaret Jensen, Pam Hayes, Aunt Alice, Aunt Helen and Aunt Anna. We were thankful for their love and support. I slept on a love seat in Bernice's room.

November 1. Bernice tried water with ginger ale. They did three blood samples. Potassium was low. It was being administered through the IV. Another medication for ulcers had been helpful.

November 2. Surgeons Miller and Litwin came again to check Bernice. She was impressed with Dr. Litwin's bedside manner. She felt cheered and comforted after his visit, rather than apprehensive. He ordered a barium swallow and X-ray, which made me apprehensive. Bernice's abdomen became distended and painful. Eventually, she threw up and got rid of the barium. Great relief. Millie Rowluck came on the bus that night to relieve me.

Wonderful. No ulcers showed on the X-ray. Bernice's stomach problem was still a mystery. We were on a strange sidetrack, but God was aware of us.

November 3. Orders were to eat a little and sit up. The horizontal position seemed to aggravate the problem. Bernice complained of pressure in the stomach. Phone calls from cousins Jim and Bettie Jacobson and Aunt Helen. The sitting up strategy seemed to work, for that period of time. What diagnostic deductions could we make from that clue?

November 4. We both had a better sleep. Bernice had porridge for breakfast and felt well enough to watch TV. However, the stomach revolted again as soon as she lay down. Dr. Worobetz from G.I. department came to consult. Dr. Rudachyk told us the evidence seemed to point to a stricture at the stomach's outlet.

November 5. Bernice slept on her right side as per orders. No upsets during the night. The X-ray showed a pooling of barium in the lower part of the stomach. They wanted to suction it out but the tube wouldn't go down. Poor Bernice. She sat stoically on the edge of the bed doing her best to co-operate. Alternately, there was talk of a surgical by-pass into the stomach. This was a Job experience for Bernice. Jesus once said to Peter, "I have prayed for you that your faith will stand the test." *Pray for us too, sweet Jesus.* Carroll Birkland was coming to stay two nights with Bernice.

November 7. Bernice had a visit from the Great Physician during the night. Her stomach was re-arranged. The gastro-intestinal tract clicked into gear. The vomiting stopped. X-rays showed barium moving out. Thank God. Visitors shared in the good news: Dorothy and John Gray, Pastor Keith and Aunt Gladys. Carroll stayed another night with Bernice while I shared chicken soup and relaxation with the Ganes family. Our hearts overflowed with gratitude.

November 8. I arrived at the hospital at 10:15, Carroll left for home. Bless her heart. Bernice had a better night. IV discontinued. Some fluid retention from lack of movement. The leg is still taut and sore. Friends from the college and career group and the mission came by to encourage. Mona brought cheery little notes from her Awana class. Things were looking up, sore leg notwithstanding.

November 9. Bernice was up several times to the bathroom. This was such a positive development that we didn't mind disturbed sleep. Pastor Lees and Myrna called. Cousin Lorelie came to pray and encourage. Brought a vibrator to stimulate circulation.

November 10. Busy morning: X-ray of the leg, stretcher shower and shampoo. Students from Bethany Bible College dropped in. Doreen stayed overnight with Bernice. Uncle Joe came for me and I had a good sleep.

November 11. We went to the sixth floor to hear the Singing Hills, who were sharing prayer and song for Bernice and Vi Gossen, a patient. Doug took Bernice to the gift shop to buy a birthday gift for Caroline, a blind girl in the next room. They gave her a bell. Cousin Cathy, Uncle Art and Aunt Anna visited in the afternoon. Thank you, Lord, for faithful folk who love and help and pray. We are lifted on wings of grace.

November 12. Last night was hectic with sore hip and elbow. Tried an ice-pack and Tylenol, with some relief. Helen Fossen from Birch Hills stayed overnight with Bernice. We appreciate our nurse friends, Millie, Carroll and Helen for their professional care and love.

November 13. Helen went home on the bus. A student doctor interviewed Bernice regarding her disease. He was interested in research, he said. Bless him for his concern. We had a very distressing night; pain and discomfort. Bernice cried, I cried. *Lord, we cling to You, for we know You are here with us.*

November 14. Dr. Rudachyk told us Bernice could be transferred to Birch Hills hospital soon. A sedative in the afternoon helped her sleep.

The next morning Jan came to finish the addresses for the Christmas letter. The swelling seemed to be receding. Thank God.

Our diary ended abruptly as we made plans to move again. Cas Bawolin volunteered to take Bernice in his motor home, while Pastor Keith and I were attendants. Cozily ensconced in blankets, Bernice was quite excited to be going back to home territory. Everyone rallied to get her on a stretcher and carried into the hospital. She got a private room with all amenities, which included local nurses who were old friends. Thank you, Cas and Pastor Keith, for your prayers and practical help; many thanks to the University Hospital staff and doctors for your concern and care.

Now we begin a new chapter in the saga of Bernice's journey with You, Lord. We proceed one day at a time. We can't see beyond today, but You have the future mapped. We'll walk with You.

Bernice's devotional calendar reminded us of Moses' struggle with doubt when he cried out to God, "Why has Thou afflicted Thy servant?" (Num. 11:11). David also asked many questions, but arrived at the answer in the stillness of his heart, "I know, O Lord, that Thy judgments are right."

Be still my soul: the Lord is on thy side;
Bear patiently the cross of grief or pain;
Leave to thy God to order and provide;
In every change He faithful will remain.

—K. Von Schlegel

■ ■ ■

We settled into our new routine. I could be at home and sleep in my own bed. What a joy to see Bernice gradually improving. We spent meal times together and afternoons "working." The Christmas letter was prepared for mailing; last minute notes and greetings in Bernice's own hand. She had dictated that letter late in October with help from Jan and her photocopier. It sounded quite matter-of-fact and cheerful. There was only passing reference to the trying experiences of the past months. Her name means victorious.

As the envelopes were filled and addressed, we offered a prayer for each dear friend.

Dr. Moolla, fascinated by his new patient with the strange disease, often called in to chat.

One day, Cheryl and Shawn appeared at the door. Hugs and kisses and exclamations! I went home to make dinner and we ate with Bernice in the lounge. Such fun.

The swelling in Bernice's leg gradually subsided, but as before, calcium remained, leaving her range of motion severely affected. No longer able to bend her leg at right angles at the hip, she had to sit on a cushion in a sloping fashion. Fortunately, her pain and discomfort eased. We had to accept that life would be different for Bernice now. Another freedom lost, she could no longer walk.

Birch Hills hospital served as a healing half-way house for us... comforting and familiar. Three years before Bernice had occupied the same bed, recuperating from a fall in our home. She had stumbled on a rug and ruptured a kidney. One year after that, in another room, Tom bade farewell to this world. In our times of extremity we have found peace and healing for the heart as well as the body within those walls.

On December 15, Bernice came home. She yearned for normalcy again. Home would be the place to start: get up in the morning, get dressed, make plans, phone somebody, catch up on life.

She was carried into the house and placed in the easy chair. "Welcome home, Bernice. We made it through the wilderness, wounded, but stronger in spirit. God promises to be with us through the fire and the flood. He was there."

"Mom, this is what I'd call a sharp turn in the road, a long detour. God must have something completely different in mind for me. We'll wait and see. Make us a cup of tea, OK, Mom?"

Bringing her home was the right thing to do. Her body and mind had been on high alert for so long. Now she could relax in the warmth of home and God's peace.

We knew, of course, the scene had changed. We couldn't pick up the action where we had left off and carry on as before. Bernice couldn't walk. Fortunately, she was petite, only 65 pounds. "Weight-bearing exercise, Mom," she chimed in cheerfully. "Good for the osteoporosis!"

By trial and error we developed our morning strategy. Below the belt dressing was done in bed. Next, lift and swing the legs over the side of the bed to finish dressing. Bernice had good taste. She chose co-ordinating clothing and accessories for herself and me. "That blouse doesn't go, Mom, pink would be better."

With firm support Bernice could walk, slowly and labouriously. We realized the importance of encouraging this mobility. I walked backwards, holding her hands, to the bathroom, to the living room, to the den to watch TV. A bedpan on a chair saved a few steps during the night. We borrowed a wheelchair from the hospital for a while, but later obtained one from the Saskatchewan Association for Independent Living. The cordless telephone, her "security blanket," rested in the curve of her arm.

Her shower bath required two attendants, one to hold, the other to wield the wash cloth efficiently and quickly before her legs gave out. Aunt Alice and Millie helped a few times, but for the long haul we contacted Home Care. Ardith was assigned to us, and for the next few months we looked forward to her weekly visit. After the bath, we enjoyed a cup of tea and a chat, Bernice's long hair spread over a towel on the back of her chair.

Aunt Alice and Bertha Opseth shared Christmas Eve with us, Norwegian style with lefse and fish. We played Bernice's favourite tapes. Before long, letters arrived every day. These loving messages energized Bernice with renewed joy and hope. Since the computer still resided at Doreen's in Saskatoon, I took on the role of secretary. Bernice managed short notes by hand.

Life went on. Can it be that we are adjusting so soon to the dramatic changes in our lifestyle? If so, we thank God.

He giveth more grace when the burdens grow greater,
He sendeth more strength when the labors increase;
To added affliction He addeth His mercy
To multiplied trials, His multiplied peace.

—A.J. Flint

The wounds, however, were not far below the surface. One day we were sorting some things from Bernice's desk in Saskatoon. Her daily calendar showed October 12, 1989. Bernice looked at it a long time. "That's when my life came to an end," she said. "No, Bernice, you don't really believe that. You said it is a sharp turn in the road. God has another plan. He knows all about this." We cried a little for dreams that had to be set aside. We thanked God for the assurance there are new dreams in the future. Then we made some tea and turned the calendar to January, 1990.

Our friend, Dr. L. Rudachyk, arranged for us to visit her at the Parkridge Centre in Saskatoon so Bernice could be fitted for a foam-in-place seat in her wheelchair. The technician carved and sculpted a block of foam until it conformed to Bernice's sloping sitting posture. Someone with a measuring tape made a few deft calculations, and before long, a stretch cover added a fine, professional finish. Feet firmly planted on the foot rests, Bernice could keep herself from sliding forward. A seat belt provided the final touch.

It was a long and tiring procedure, involving two trips to Saskatoon and many fittings. A resigned look on her face, Bernice smiled bravely and observed, "I guess we have a choice of two reactions now, Mom: 'Oh, God, has it come to this?' or 'This is great! We're mobile and comfortable! Thank You, God and all Your good helpers here!'"

We were both encouraged by this first small step in the recovery of freedom and independence. The seat, in two parts, could be removed and the wheelchair folded for transport in the car. Foam slabs provided support for her in the passenger seat which reclined as needed. Yes, we were mobile again!

These excursions to Saskatoon afforded opportunities to renew friendships. We called on Doug and Heather, Cheryl, Brian and Angie, and the Mission. Some places were not really accessible, but we didn't give up easily. Seeing these friends after that long wilderness journey seemed a little strange, like coming back from the dead, needing to find that familiar spark again. It was part of the process of learning to live again.

That learning received a tremendous boost when Cheryl and Shawn announced their wedding date in August. Theirs was a romantic story. They met and fell in love in Vancouver after Cheryl's car accident which resulted in her loss of sight. She never saw her man, but she knew him by voice and touch, big and strong and kind. Many prayed for restoration of her sight. Shawn, droll and practical, spoke privately to God. "Wait until after we're married, Lord. She may not like what she sees."

CHAPTER SEVEN

Opportunity Beckons

In early summer a new idea was planted in our minds. The Home Care co-ordinator told us about her daughter, presently recovering from an accident. Her doctor had referred her to Wascana Rehabilitation Centre (WRC) in Regina for therapy. Very pleased with the results, she wondered if anything could be done for Bernice. Knowing so well the nature of this disease, we had our doubts, but Bernice saw other possibilities.

"Mom, Karen lives there, Aunt Margaret and Uncle Jim live there. Shawn is thinking of Bible college there. How about that? Maybe this is the open door we've been waiting for!" Her eyes shone.

When we contacted WRC, Dr. Milo Fink, the medical director, suggested that Bernice come for an assessment. He agreed that her boney deposits could not be reversed, but saw possibilities for improving her mobility and function. He offered to let her live in the permanent residence.

She spent a few days in the rehab department to acquaint herself with the building and be reviewed in Occupational Therapy for possibilities.

WRC is a beautiful building. We strolled along the concourse, pointing and exclaiming like tourists at the Taj Mahal. The architect, bless him, created an atmosphere of space, beauty and peace. We sensed order and efficiency everywhere. It was not until much later that we realized the complexity of services and programs housed within these walls, but even in the course of our brief investigative tours, we saw evidence of activity: children in pint-sized wheelchairs, an injured worker nursing a broken limb, stroke victims learning to cope. Regulars from the war veterans department socialized in the cafeteria. In the extended care wing, where Bernice would live, we met several younger residents, living and pursuing their interests among the elderly who lived nearby, a cross section of life on the fourth level.

The Centre's mission statement warmed our hearts:

Wascana Rehabilitation Centre is
dedicated to helping individuals with
a disability achieve the greatest level
of personal independence and quality of life.

Dr. Fink asked the OT workshop to come up with ways for Bernice to function more independently. What inventive ideas. We finally settled for a "standing table" of appropriate height, with velcro support at her back, enabling her to feed herself and write. When completed, the table would be shipped to Birch Hills. We went home in good spirits, thankful to God for arranging this "open door" for us.

August came, and with it the long-awaited wedding. What a fabulous affair! We watched with tears as Cheryl walked down the aisle with her brother, who gave her to Shawn, her big, strong man. Bernice composed a poem which she read during the ceremony, "Love is like a rose." She stood in her finery, leaning against the back of the wheelchair, just long enough to recite her poem and present a rose to the nearest bridesmaid.

As guests gathered for the reception, Bernice glanced eagerly about, looking for familiar faces. Doreen sat with us. Betty and Ester and many others stopped to chat. It was a fun evening of music, speeches and laughter. Bernice posed for pictures with the newlyweds. She bade them a wistful good-bye.

"It won't be the same now that you are married, Cheryl. You're my special friend... the wind beneath my wings. We won't let that be changed. We need each other."

Amid hugs and tears they vowed to keep their friendship close forever.

In time, the swelling in Bernice's leg disappeared, but the muscle became weak and calcified. Both legs were permanently flexed at the hips and knees, resulting in a very limited range of motion. Walking with bent knees and hips was labourious and exhausting. She slept on her side, a small cushion between her knees. A soft pillow filled the cavity in her back. Due to calcification in her growing years, her torso developed a tilt. Her left elbow was fixed a quarter inch from her body, and care was needed to prevent pressure ulcers. A pillow at her head had to be tucked just so for the comfort of that stiff neck and another pillow supported her left foot, as it tended to drop. There now, all tucked in. A word from the Lord, a prayer, a kiss and lights out.

Four hours later, bathroom call. Dismantle the pillow fort, use the bedpan, have a drink, turn to the other side and re-tuck. Always a smile. "Thanks, Mom."

What is it like to be helpless? "I used to run and walk and get out of bed by myself," Bernice sighed. "Now I can hardly remember what is was like. I see people jump out of their chairs and go. Something leaps within me but there is no response in my body. Yet, I am in here, whole and healthy, waiting for my release, however God wants to do it."

At 65 pounds, Bernice seemed, to the casual observer, a pitiable sight, a deformed skeleton, barely able to move. What could she possibly contribute to society? By current reasoning, she was a liability. But to us who loved her and were loved by her, she was beautiful. Her shining eyes and quick smile illuminated her face. That whole person who lived inside the body shone through those eyes, spoke sanctified wisdom through her lips and directed her in many loving deeds of kindness. We were quite unaware of the outer shell. It was there but it didn't matter. We learned to know *her* as a fabulous, fun person who inspired us upward and onward by her positive, unselfish attitude. Her presence was enough to rebuke any unworthy thought or word. She was a messenger of God, sent to live with us for a while. A short while, but long enough to accomplish God's purpose. We had long ceased thinking of Bernice as "crippled." She referred to herself as a whole person living in a dysfunctional body. Now we learn that handicapped has a negative connotation, though "living victoriously with a handicap" might be acceptable. Disabled as an adjective didn't really sit well either, but *PERSON* with a disability fit the picture perfectly.

Bernice's friends, Tim and Darlene, shared the following article with me. I found that it well illustrates the extent of unconditional love, that lavish, heart hungry, unreasonable outpouring of devotion which asks nothing in return other than acceptance. Any child who has loved a toy to shreds understands this. Such is God's love to us, asking nothing in return but our acceptance.

The Velveteen Rabbit

"What is REAL?" asked the Rabbit one day when they were lying side by side near the nursery guard rail, before Nana came to tidy the room. "Does it mean having things that buzz inside you and a stick-out handle?"

"Real isn't how you are made," said the Skin Horse. "It's a thing that happens to you. When a child loves you for a long, long time, not just to play with, but REALLY loves you, then you become Real."

"Does it hurt?" asked the Rabbit.

"Sometimes," said the Skin Horse, for he was always truthful. "When you are Real you don't mind being hurt."

"Does it happen all at once, like being wound up," he asked, "or bit by bit?"

"It doesn't happen all at once," said the Skin Horse. "You become. It takes a long time. That's why it doesn't often happen to people who break easily, or have sharp edges, or who have to be carefully kept. Generally, by the time you are Real, most of your hair has been loved off, and your eyes drop out and you get loose in the joints and very shabby. But these things don't matter at all, because once you are Real you can't be ugly, except to people who don't understand."

—Margery Williams

What is the measure of our worth? God loves us. I remember Bernice's reaction to a grade ten Social Studies lesson. It was the lifeboat theory on survival. The boat was overloaded and someone had to be eliminated. Judgments were made according to age, health and education. Bernice was highly indignant. We felt a chill in our soul. What's going on here? Has human reasoning brought us to the point where we can, at our convenience, preserve or discard a life? When abortion becomes acceptable, is euthanasia far behind? It's a gradual process of deadening our senses to the value of life.

We were created by God and received from Him the spark of life. Scientists have produced many wonders, but they have not duplicated life, that indefinable, spiritual something which governs the intricacies of the human organism. "We are fearfully and wonderfully made" (Ps. 139:14). The Creator endowed us with the seed of eternal life, and our destiny is to return to Him who gave it.

"And God said, Let us make man in our image, after our likeness..." (Gen. 1:26).

"And the Lord God formed man of the dust of the ground, and breathed into his nostrils the breath of life; and man became a living soul" (Gen. 2:7).

■ ■ ■

In January, 1991, we received a phone call from Wascana Rehabilitation Centre. "We have a bed for Bernice, available immediately. How soon can she be here?"

Whoa! Hold on a minute. We have to think about this. Travelling in winter, wondering about what and how much to pack; getting into the moving mode again. We persuaded WRC to allow us a little more time, but in just three days, we were set to go. Lewis Reid offered to transport us in his van, and Frank Rowluck sat in the co-pilot's seat. In addition to a makeshift bed to keep Bernice comfortable, the van accommodated an easy chair, all the luggage, the wheelchair, the dismantled table and me.

Thinking about the open door of opportunity before us, we experienced a variety of emotions: excitement, apprehension, wonder, gratitude, sadness, wistfulness. After a year at home, Bernice had established a few roots again, certainly in my heart, but she felt the urge to try her wings again.

Our kind chauffeurs landed us safely at the impressive front entrance of 2180-23rd Avenue in Regina, Bernice's new home.

Main 5, Room 529. We unpacked sufficiently to feel at home. The bed was re-made with our foam pads, soft pillows and Bernice's favourite bedspread. After supper I went to the Brown's to spend the night. I planned to stay several days to aid the orientation process... hers and mine.

Bernice met her neighbours, Jil, Connie, Brad and Del, who were residents her own age. Others were older, some bed patients, others able to sit in a chair during the day.

Every day was a learning experience, indeed an eye-opener. These young survivors were positive thinkers, aggressive and optimistic.

In visiting her new friends, Bernice discovered they all used computers, and being quadriplegic, they had devised a unique method of communicating: "sip and puff." A drinking straw attached to an extension gooseneck arm enabled the operator to blow Morse Code signals which translated into text on the screen. A sip is a dot and a puff is a dash. We watched in amazement as Connie demonstrated that her no-hands method compares favourably with conventional typing if not for speed, but certainly for results.

Bernice was encouraged to try this method, but she decided to carry on with the limited use of her hands, now much more limited due to her sitting posture. She thought her protruding teeth might make it too difficult to hold the straw. Eventually, a smaller keyboard on a goose-neck attachment enabled her to function quite well.

Uncle Jim built a computer desk for her, a multi-functional piece which accommodated vast amounts of software as well as plain "stuff." We had fun tidying and decorating. The standing table, placed in the dining room, enabled her to feed herself. Before long she met Ernie, volunteer extraordinare, whose wife had been a Wascana resident until her death. He could be spotted on the premises almost every day, running errands and quietly performing small miracles for residents.

The need for a motorized chair became evident almost immediately. Otherwise, Bernice had to sit and wait to be pushed. Fortunately, the OT people located a used one which could be adjusted to fit Bernice's steering hand, and her custom wheelchair cushions easily transferred from one chair to the other as needed. Now, this was real mobility! The Para-transit bus system enhanced her mobility even further: anywhere in the city for a buck and ten. The Golden Mile Shopping Centre beckoned. Friends were within reach. Some time later, the Saskatchewan Transportation Company purchased two intercity buses equipped with hydraulic lifts for wheelchair passengers. Even the washroom was wheelchair accessible, a concept so new that regular passengers sometimes felt insecure in all that space! Bernice found this bus an ideal way to travel home for visits. She sat like a queen at the back of the bus, reading a favourite book. STC is to be commended for their vision and concern.

Shawn and Cheryl had moved to Regina shortly after their wedding to prepare for his seminary studies at Canadian Bible College. Bernice had hardly unpacked when they burst into her room in a flurry of excitement. Happy days are here again! Upstairs in the cafeteria they made plans. Shopping, of course. Cheryl followed the motorized chair around the mall and together they decided on colours, styles, fragrances and cappuccino flavours. Occasionally, they went out for supper using Shawn's truck. He carried Bernice into the building and propped her in a corner while Cheryl followed, holding onto his elbow. Shawn, affable as always, served up suitable portions for his two girls.

As time went on, other girls joined the family. In June, Sarah was born and the following year, Rachel. Grandma came to help, but Cheryl amazed us by her adjustment to mothering in the dark. Shawn integrated babysitting with theology and found them complementary on many points.

Outings with Bernice had to be curtailed for a while. Instead, she visited them in their second-floor apartment. Shawn carried her up the stairs. When Sarah was a few months old, it seemed timely to try shopping again, but how to manage the logistics of such a venture? Papa was busy with theology, but one of the moms could be counted on to show up quite often. Such a visit triggered a flurry of phone calls.

"Hi, Cheryl! Mom is coming today. Do you want to go shopping tomorrow?"

We spent the afternoon cruising the mall. Mom pushed the stroller. Cappuccino stops were timed to coincide with Sarah's nursing schedule. Shawn met us at a pre-determined spot, and Bernice and I went home on the Para-transit bus. A satisfactory outing. Now to examine our purchases.

Bernice missed her Sunday church time, so much a part of her life before. Local clergy conducted weekly services in the chapel but it wasn't the same as a church home. We talked at length about her search for a place of spiritual fellowship and refreshment. She had some stipulations: It had to be a place where the Bible is faithfully preached and taught. It had to be wheelchair accessible and user friendly, and it had to be near enough to be reached by Para-transit in time for the service. This last was a stickler since the buses are busy on Sundays.

After several tries she met someone from Harvest City Church, a most interesting group of believers. They had purchased a school building which uniquely suited their needs. Grades K to 12 were taught in the classrooms, which on Sundays doubled as Sunday School rooms. The gym became a sanctuary as chairs were set up and musicians took their places. Bernice noticed a good number of early arrivers gathered in the library to pray for the service. She was impressed. Pastor Dave Wells welcomed her and there were smiles and handshakes as others introduced themselves.

She was further impressed to learn that a shuttle bus schedule had been arranged which eliminated the problem of early bookings with Para-transit. Randy from second floor was already a regular at Harvest City. "Wow!" she thought. "I can handle this. Thank You, Lord, for another open door."

Several friends from Harvest City had offered to chauffeur the WRC volunteer van on Sunday mornings. "We'll get you to the church on time!" Bernice and Randy became good friends. Dear Randy, whose heart overflowed with the joy of the Lord, but who had to struggle to express himself. Bernice soon learned to "hear" him. They sat near the front of the church, taking it all in. On my frequent visits I shared the van ride and worship service with them.

Picture an orchestra and a worship team with be-ribboned tambourines leading the song service. With such inspiration, even the most lackluster voice could be motivated. The lyrics were on the overhead and the singing of others carried you along. Her face shining, Bernice clapped gently to the beat. Then Pastor Dave, faithful and well-loved shepherd of the flock, shared a message from the Bible, illustrated occasionally with humourous comments on the human condition. Chuckles and "amens" could be heard.

Bernice joined one of several home Bible study groups, where she made many enduring friendships: Tim and Darlene, Grace, Julie, Barb and others. She had found a church home.

Over time, a few creature comforts were added to her room: the TV, a necessity for relaxation and change of pace; the VCR, for after all, one must have choice; a stereo cassette player. With dozens of tapes to choose from, it was hum time, even snap the fingers time. The trick was to catch someone walking by who might change the tapes for her, or do any number of things that require hands and feet. The regular staff, bless them, had enough to do with care and cleaning.

WRC provided many, many opportunities for volunteers. Of course, there has always been a need for helping hands, but watching eager young people like Bernice direct their lives and projects from the wheelchair inspired me to join the team. On one of my visits, within ten minutes of entering Bernice's room, I was asked to scratch her head, open mail, change a tape and reheat coffee.

By any stretch of our imagination, can we picture ourselves immobilized? What feelings of panic, fear, frustration and discouragement must be faced and conquered? What a challenge to us who have hands and feet, who have eyes and ears and understanding to share. Let me be to you what you need. Let me draw from you the essence of courage under fire, so both of us shall be enlarged in spirit.

Securing a personal helper at WRC was one's own responsibility. Family members appeared daily to assist with meals. Jil's parents, with years of experience, were involved in everything from correspondence to building furniture. Smiling Sherry often brought her daughter Ashley for therapy, thereby hearing of others' needs and so becoming a volunteer. Connie, always working on complex projects, needed someone to run and fetch. Sometimes, in a pinch, she appeared at Bernice's door. "May I borrow your mom for a little while?" Then we would both go, though Bernice was loathe to miss a phone call.

These girls were paragons of order and good housekeeping. We knew that the moms and other volunteers did the actual arranging, but under explicit direction from the manager in the wheelchair. They instructed as to the exact whereabouts of everything in their room; the contents of every file and every drawer. That measure of control was vital to those who lived in an unresponsive body, those who directed the course of their days from the executive office of the mind and heart.

Bernice, far from being a demanding person, followed the scriptural injunction to consider others' needs before her own. She sought to have the mind of Christ and practiced it. She was a joy to serve.

Jesus Himself modeled selflessness and servanthood as a principle of life, a concept that transcended the golden rule. True servanthood serves with patient humility and love, asking nothing in return except the heavenly Father's pleasure. Jesus taught His disciples in John 13 to cultivate such a mind set. Is it possible, joined as we are to rebellious flesh, to achieve this goal? *Lord, please teach me this gentle way of unconditional love, free of encumbrances and expectations, free of the distracting need to be appreciated, where Your pleasure is enough.*

That radiant
smile appeared
early.

Brian and Bernice—
togetherness.

Birthdays
were special

"Hi, Mom!"

School days begin.

pichzr of me

Self-portrait

Mom and Dad with Bernice.

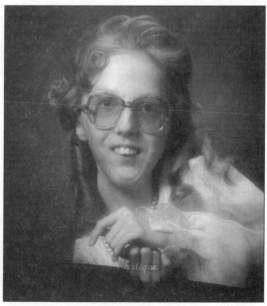

Graduation

With Mom, Brian, Angie and family.

Doug and Heather Powell, Mark and Tamara
—faithful caregivers.

Shawn and Cheryl's wedding.

Shawn, Cheryl and children.

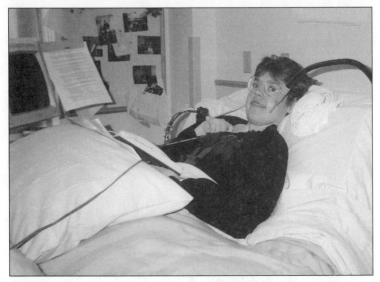

Connie at work

Independence '92 in Vancouver,
World Congress on Disability.

Off to YWAM in
Salem, Oregon.

With Moira Brown at
100 Huntley Street.

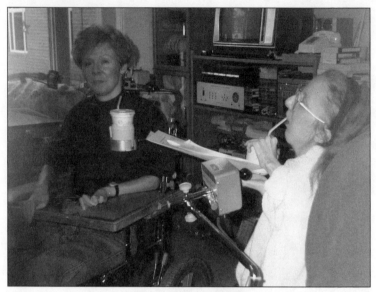

Consulting with Jil.

Dear friends Connie and Sherry.

CHAPTER EIGHT

Back to School

Connie became a close friend and confidante. They cruised the hallway visiting each other, sharing problems, feelings, their faith, their prayers. Connie, an experienced resident, helped Bernice adjust to a new lifestyle. Her boldness inspired Bernice to launch out, to go for it. She found it both encouraging and intimidating that Connie had already earned a university degree. As they discussed possibilities, the thought of attending university was daunting. Expending all that effort, Bernice reasoned, would have to be worthwhile and rewarding. "It must contribute to my spiritual as well as intellectual understanding, so I can serve my Lord better," she added. After much thought, she decided correspondence courses would be more appropriate.

Those courses were daunting enough. For starters, she chose psychology and counseling from Alberta's Athabasca University. "To help me understand myself and others," she explained. Later, she joined Cheryl for evening classes at Canadian Bible College. A dozen or more student wives and others participated in SEAN... Study by Extension for All Nations. Eventually, they covered books one to six of "A Compendium of Pastoral Theology... the life of Christ in the book of Matthew." Though it was a credit course, Bernice and Cheryl declined to be pressured with deadlines. They talked and absorbed and enjoyed. Marlene Morrison, a fellow student, encouraged them in their quest.

Eager to find out what psychology from a Christian point of view might be like, Bernice ordered "Introduction to Psychology" by Paul Magnus, a professor at Briercrest Bible College. I took on a little extra enlightenment in the process of reading and re-reading with Bernice.

Almost overwhelmed by the volume of information to be read and analyzed, she determined to retain only what was positive and helpful. She read Gary Belkin's "Introduction to Counseling." Glancing through that book, I now see passages highlighted, with comments or question marks in the margins. While she got used to her new mini keyboard, a friend typed her assignments.

We discussed the development of psychology, turning up such names as William James, B.F. Skinner, Sigmund Freud, Carl Jung, Victor Frankl. For all their wisdom, most of them ignored, or were unaware of, the spiritual dimension of man. They probed deeply into the development of body and mind from birth, or even conception, to death; a short journey. Without assurance of ongoing life after death, it is surely a hopeless journey. Bernice sorted through these philosophical discussions and emerged even more convinced that "the Word of our God shall stand forever" (Isa. 40:8) and that we, too, are destined for eternity.

Bernice launched enthusiastically into her studies. Her first assignment set the pace for the demanding task ahead: "Explain fully why a Christian should or should not study psychology, give scriptural support, drawing your ideas from your course text, textbooks and the Bible."

Bernice's answer:

All truth is God's truth. Secular psychology is usually thought to be science pursuing its own course without regard for God. That is usually true. But, as in other sciences, their studies often turn up basic, irrefutable facts. Therefore, as a Christian, I should investigate and be aware of what is being taught, distinguishing every truth that bears the imprint of God the Creator from even a shade of error. To do this, one must know God, know His Word and be enlightened by the Holy Spirit.

A knowledge of psychology and the inner workings of the mind broadens our understanding of the deep root of sin and the need for redemption.

"The heart is deceitful above all things, and desperately wicked: who can know it?" (Jer. 17:9).

Also, it enhances self-understanding. According to Matthew 7:3-5 we usually find it easier to judge others than ourselves. "And why beholdest thou the mote that is in thy brother's eye, but considerest not the beam that is in thine own eye...."

Sharing the Apostle Paul's frustrating experience with the old nature brings home the subtle reactions of the flesh. "For I know that in me (that is, in my flesh,) dwelleth no good thing: for to will is present with me; but how to perform that which is good I find not" (Rom. 7:18).

"For to be carnally minded is death; but to be spiritually

minded is life and peace. Because the carnal mind is enmity against God: for it is not subject to the law of God, neither indeed can be" (Rom. 8:6-7).

Thank God there is victory through Jesus Christ our Lord (Rom. 7:24-25).

In understanding ourselves, we are better equipped to deal with others. We are encouraged to be less judgmental and impatient with the behaviour and personality problems we see in others. It enables us to look for possible causes why people act and react the way they do. The biblical exhortations to "uphold one another, love one another, forgive one another" add the dimension of Christian understanding to our interpersonal relationships.

"Forbearing one another, and forgiving one another, if any man have a quarrel against any: even as Christ forgave you, so also do ye" (Col. 3:13).

Another reason for cultivating a wider knowledge of psychology is to prepare us to deal with the questions of others. It's good to know what other people think so we are not caught unawares. For this reason, it's also important to keep up to date on current psychological trends. In counseling, it is often the case that people respond more positively to Bible teaching on their problems if they can see from a logical, natural point of view that their choices and lifestyle are detrimental. Of course, the Bible, being God's book, is perfectly logical and apropos but this is not apparent to the natural man, who "receiveth not the things of the Spirit of God for they are foolishness unto him" (1 Cor. 2:14).

A sincere, thinking person will see the truth of these verses from Scripture: "He that soweth to his flesh shall of the flesh reap corruption" (Gal. 6:8). "There is a way that seemeth right unto a man, but the end thereof are the ways of death" (Prov. 14:12).

A knowledge of psychology also contributes to the efficiency of the Church's work. Research findings regarding learning, communication and persuasion can help in outreach, evangelism and missionary work. The study of motivation, emotion and the psychology of adjustment can aid in the preparation of missionaries to enter new cultures. There is a danger, however, that we can depend more on methods and man's wisdom than the leading of the Holy Spirit.

A Christian philosophy of psychology must begin and end with the Bible. According to William Kirwan:

> To cope with our own emotional problems as well as those of others, we need to understand something about the cause of such problems. The biblical picture of human creation and the subsequent fall into sin explains how mental anguish and psychological difficulties became part of our existence. Even though the Bible is not a psychology textbook, it informs us how we came to be the complicated emotional persons we are. In fact, the Bible's teachings contain in embryonic (and sometimes more fully developed) form all the valid teachings of modern behavioral science.
>
> —*Biblical Concepts for Christian Counseling,*
> *Grand Rapids: Baker*

■ ■ ■

Bernice was experiencing difficulty with her printer. The exasperation level rose until it was agreed that the whole system should be replaced. The prospect of obtaining a new computer enhanced her enthusiasm to get on with her courses and other writing. A provincial agency,

Vocational Rehabilitation for Disabled Persons (VRDP), agreed to grant her the use of a new computer and laser printer plus WordPerfect and other software. The mini keyboard provided access to this exciting new tool. She was thrilled. Staff member Anne Bartel, a real encourager, contributed advice and guidance. VRDP also assisted financially with some of Bernice's courses, all of which she sincerely appreciated. She often called me to report on her latest achievement.

A wide array of software enabled her to create banners, posters, greeting cards and designs for projects. The temptation to explore fun things often called for the exercise of discipline.

A voracious reader, Bernice shaped her philosophy, and nurtured her need to grow in knowledge and wisdom, by the books she chose. The Bible placed first on her list. From there she adopted Christ's principle: "Thou shalt love the Lord thy God with all thy heart... [and] thy neighbour as thyself" (Mark 12:30-31).

Luci Swindoll's book, *Wide My World, Narrow My Bed*, opened Bernice's eyes to the vast sisterhood of single women everywhere, and the opportunities of ministry by them and for them.

Margaret Jensen's series of warm, inspirational books moved her to see God working behind the scenes in everyday situations. Her long distance link with the author encouraged her to dream of being a writer.

Most motivating of all were Joni Eareckson Tada's writings: Bernice readily related to her disability and her search for spiritual significance in the midst of adversity. These books, *Secret Strength, Glorious Intruder, When is it Right to Die?, Heaven, Your Real Home,* contributed much to

Bernice's insight to her own struggle.

The texts from her psychology classes, though required reading, were not equally meaningful to her. Some show more evidence of use and contemplation: *Emotions—Can You Trust Them?* (Dr. James Dobson) encourages careful analysis of one's feelings; *Walls of My Heart* (Dr. Bruce Thompson) on breaking out and being free; *Dropping Your Guard* (Charles R. Swindoll) deals with open relationships; *The Sensation of Being Somebody* (Maurice E. Wagner) shares insights into boosting one's self image; *Ordering Your Private World* (Gordon MacDonald) on inner order and self appraisal. All contributed to the development of Bernice's philosophy of life.

For a change of pace and relaxation, Bernice liked Bodie Thoene's *Zion Covenant* series.

She felt her calling from the Lord to be an intercessor, to pray for others: Christian leaders, government leaders, family and friends. She wrote to the prime minister and to the Saskatchewan premier, assuring them of her prayers that they would receive wisdom and guidance in their weighty decisions. She proudly displayed their replies.

"Many people criticize the government," she said. "It must be encouraging for them to hear something positive. Besides, they do need God's help. If only they knew it."

Several well-thumbed books became mentors in the contest she had undertaken, for it is a battle against the forces of evil in this world: *The Prayer Shield* (C. Peter Wagner), *Spiritual Warfare* (Dean Sherman), *The Spiritual Warrior's Prayer Guide* (Quin Sherrer, Ruthanne Garlock), and *How To Meet the Enemy* (John MacArthur Jr.). All emphasized the need for prayer.

Called to Care by Chester Custer and *Improving Your Serve* by Charles Swindoll spoke of Bernice's desire to be that servant to others with special needs. She often reminded us, "Everyone has a handicap of some kind. On some of us it shows. Lord, let me be Your love extended to those who need it."

Christmas Holidays

How we spent our Christmas holidays over the years proved to be a measure of how much people loved us and cared for us. Travelling home for Christmas could be hazardous, Saskatchewan winters being what they are, so one year we decided to stay in Regina for the holiday. Keen for a change of scene, Bernice accepted an offer from the Browns to use their home while they visited family in Toronto. To make the season more festive, she invited a few friends. Norm and Marlene Morrison with daughter Karen, students at Canadian Bible College, were new in town. Laura and Wayne Johnston from Harvest City had no definite plans. They agreed to come. We had fun planning Christmas dinner. Para-transit took us to the mall where we found a turkey and all necessities to go with it.

Uncle Jim had set up a lighted tree on the patio. We found a tablecloth in Margaret's linen closet, and Norm got the fireplace going. The ambiance of Christmas, home and friends enveloped us in warmth. Dinner over, we visited and played games. Norm, the seminary student, shared the Word of God and led us in prayer. A perfect Christmas. Thank You, Lord.

The Browns had suggested we use their king-size bed, complete with soft, wooly mattress cover. We slept well for several nights and ate leftovers by day. We tidied up, did the laundry and left for our next appointment with thankful hearts. Connie's mom, Carol Oxelgren, had invited us for New Year's dinner with their family. Bernice, of course, had spent time with the Oxelgren's before. For me it was an opportunity to meet Connie's family—sister Lisa and many others.

The following year, Jil's parents, Barb and Jack Harker, invited us to their home for Christmas. We shared a lovely meal, though Jack's sweet potato casserole somehow stands out in my memory. We appreciate the gracious hospitality of folks who make room for others in the circle of family fellowship.

Thinking about the New Year's weekend, Bernice had an idea. The Regina Inn offered special rates to people spending the holiday season with hospitalized family members. "We qualify," she said. So for two days we lounged, watched TV, caught up on reading, ate in the coffee shop and patronized the beauty salon. Surprise on New Year's Eve... the dining room was closed. We ordered pizza from across the street. I tried, without success, to find Guy Lombardo or Mart Kenny on TV. At midnight, the distant sounds of revelry from the street heralded the arrival of a new year. We thanked God for His care in the past year and committed the new one into His hands.

Bernice's friends, Tim and Darlene Miller, included us in their 1993 Christmas plans, along with several others. With no children of their own, they invested themselves in the lives of friends. As a member of their home Bible study group, Bernice learned to appreciate their fellowship. When Tim was transferred to Chilliwack, Bernice felt bereft. Time didn't allow for self-pity; life went on and the telephone bills went up.

In December, 1994, Darlene suggested that Bernice fly to Chilliwack to spend Christmas with them. I suffered some anguish at the thought of her flying alone. By all reports they had a ball. At one point, they decided that Bernice's sponge baths didn't quite measure up so they planned a shower. Wrapped in a towel, she was carried to the tub. Darlene, dressed in shorts, stood in the tub with her, Tim reached around the curtain to hold Bernice's arm, eyes discreetly averted. Not since rubber ducky days has there been so much hilarity in the bathtub.

Returning home, Bernice missed by hours a blizzard in Calgary which would have meant an overnight delay. "See, Mom," she chided me, "God was looking after me. I even got to sit beside a nurse."

Bernice enjoyed many supper visits with the Ehmanns, Sherry, Jim and Ashley. On one occasion I joined them for a winter barbeque. As we sat around the table, forks expectantly in hand, Jim emerged from the patio dressed in parka and boots, triumphantly bearing a platter of perfect steaks. Bernice's portion required a little attention from the mincer before she could sample his cooking. Her inability to swallow coarse food, often a source of vexation and embarrassment to her, was no problem for her friends, who were always ready to accommodate her needs.

After supper, during game time, Ashley easily outmaneuvered us all. She relished these opportunities to match wits, especially with her dad. Perched in her wheelchair, her delicate hands on the table, she analyzed every look and move. A brilliant mind operating from cramped quarters.

We marveled at their newly-remodeled, completely accessible home: expansive, tiled floor area, spacious rooms, wheelchair-level drawers, knobs, handles, tele-phone. Space and maneuverability were basic considerations for the wheelchair occupant and helper. Their home is an outstanding example of adaptation to circumstances, not merely coping with patience, but aggressively and confidently meeting obstacles head on. We shall overcome. I learned later that Bernice and Connie had contributed ideas in the planning of these renovations.

CHAPTER NINE

The Big Project, A New Beginning

In the summer of 1991, Bernice called me with an urgent request. "We're on to something big here, Mom. Connie and Jil have been commissioned to research a paper on the feasibility of individual accommodation and funding for people with disabilities. Sounds awesome, doesn't it? Ike Hammell and I are working with them. But it's such a huge undertaking, we're swamped. We need help. Could you come for a while and give us a hand?"

So I became one of several volunteers who served as hands and feet for the research team. It became an unrelenting, totally absorbing effort for them from May, 1991, to March, 1992. For the rest of us, it was an education in the intricacies of research and publishing.

The target group under consideration was persons who were eighteen years and over, who had a permanent disability, who required daily attendant services, who still had the ability to direct and supervise the assistance they required and who could manage their personal affairs.

The group's dream was to see such individuals have the opportunity to live independently with self-directed attendant services. The object of their proposal was to present a detailed study of the needs of persons living with disabilities, current services available, and a blueprint for a new and superior model of independent living. To quote from the preface of their publication: "This proposal for tailor-made attendant services is based on the first-hand experiences of persons with permanent, severe physical disabilities. Too often society chooses to see us as ill persons who need to be 'cared for,' yet we dream of living independently and in charge of our own affairs. Our desire is to live as normally as possible, to contribute something of ourselves to society."

Dozens in the target group were interviewed. Exhaustive analyses of comparative costs, accessible housing and auxiliary services added to their fund of information. Finally, a list of well-considered recommendations rested their case. Their paper, titled *A New Beginning*, was published by the South Saskatchewan Independent Living Centre (SSILC). The finished product, a very professional piece of work, received undiluted praise from their mentor and friend, Harvey Stalwick, a local educator.

The task ahead was to persuade the Saskatchewan government to consider their recommendations. They met with Louise Simard, the Minister of Health and other officials who were duly impressed with their work. A limited pilot project for one or two individuals might be feasible, they said. Unfortunately, financial austerity had begun to set in. The doughty researchers turned their attentions to other things. They were proud of their accomplishment.

We continue to look for the day when this vision for the disabled will become reality.

Independence and freedom are basic human aspirations, first evident when the child says "no" and "mine." For persons with disabilities, the need to overcome and achieve can become a driving force. It can be frustrating to reconcile this yearning with institutional living. Care facilities vary from poor to excellent. Even the best cannot escape the fact of staff and time limitations. When Bernice was obliged to wear Attends at night, she understood the practical reason for that. To deliberately urinate in bed went against every ingrained instinct, yet it was one of many small freedoms and choices that must be set aside in the name of efficiency. In time, she saw the advantage of wearing Attends during the day, on extended outings or when too much coffee created an emergency.

Bowel management didn't affect Bernice because she was small and relatively mobile. Others, who required the lift to move them from place to place, were encouraged by diet, purgatives or enemas to evacuate the bowel at specified times. One's personal inclinations must be set aside for the good of all. The dream of living independently with a caregiver on call burns like a pilot light in their hearts. An unreasonable dream? We hear of such programs in other provinces and the USA. Yet when we see conditions in some parts of the world, we cannot but be thankful for what we have. Gratitude is a healing attitude. Just the same, the pilot light continues to burn.

Several years ago, a film documentary entitled, "The Switch," appeared, based on the real life experience of an accident victim. A young man crashed his motorcycle and became a quadriplegic. On life supports, he moved from

ICU to a nursing home. Completely depressed by his environment and the hopelessness of his future, he wanted to die. Friends encouraged him with tender loving care and many technological aids. He finally persuaded a knowledgeable friend to secretly install a switch so he could disconnect his life supports. Just knowing that he had the power to choose life or death energized his will to live.

From then on, his family and friends sought to move those in authority to provide more suitable age and ability appropriate accommodation for the disabled. His father's plea before the US Senate is a classic of good sense and logic. He urged the legislators to consider the present prison population, those who have abused society and yet are cared for at taxpayers' expense and given opportunity to rehabilitate and educate themselves. In contrast, he said, there are citizens with disabilities who yearn to be given an opportunity to live with hope and to contribute the hard-won achievements of their zeal and enthusiasm. But this, he pointed out, is deemed too costly.

His plea bore fruit. His son moved into a group home with others his age who also had dreams to pursue.

Someone has observed that a society can be assessed and judged by its treatment of its most defenseless citizens.

■ ■ ■

During the winter of '92, another idea had been simmering on the back burner. With *A New Beginning* out of the way, this new opportunity leaped to the fore.

"Independence '92," the World Congress on Disability, would be held in Vancouver in April, with delegates from many countries. There was keen interest on Main 5 and 6 to be counted among them. Connie clicked into overdrive to plan and arrange. Finally, Ike, Connie and Bernice were chosen to make the trip. Funding of up to 75% was granted to them by the federal Secretary of State. Additional help came from SSILC and a local service club.

Of course, attendants had to accompany them. Ike's wife, Karen, signed on to help her husband. Connie's long-time friend, Percy Rusaw, agreed to share their adventure. Bernice persuaded her nurse friend from Birch Hills, Millie Rowluck, to come.

In preparing for this event, Vancouver went all out to accommodate its guests. Wherever they went, they were surrounded by helpful people. Accessibility and possibility became the watchwords. The elegant Waterfront Hotel included, at Connie's request, a lift to transfer her from chair to bed. New technology being demonstrated promised unheard of ability to overcome obstacles. The atmosphere was heady with excitement. We chuckled later over one souvenir they picked up: a button which boldly declared, "We demand the right to pee."

When you get right down to it, that's the bottom line. The option of choice is precious to those who find themselves so often unable to exercise it.

Bernice and Connie presented a poster display on their pet project, individual funding for attendant services. They competed for attention with dozens of workshops and technological demonstrations but were gratified that a few delegates from abroad bought copies of their proposal, *A New Beginning*.

They found time for extracurricular activities as well. Bernice arranged happy encounters with old friends from home, Beth (Lees) and Alan Balisky, Walter and Betty Ridgway, a former pastor in Wakaw, Saskatchewan. They went shopping and sightseeing, utterly amazed to find every form of transportation accessible. The girls wanted to explore, leading Percy and Millie on a merry chase. A small panic occurred one evening when they almost missed the sea bus; another panic the next day when Bernice lost her camera. Fortunately, it happened on conference premises and was returned to the lost and found.

The Congress ended, with delegates gratified for a very successful event; they were a little sad in bidding farewell to so many new friends. After unpacking and sorting her notes, Bernice summarized the conference for *Parascope*, the newsletter of the Canadian Paraplegic Association. Her article rekindles the common triumphant spirit: *we are not alone.*

INDEPENDENCE '92
The World Congress on Disability
by Bernice Boyes

The City of Vancouver will never be the same. From April 21-25, over 7,000 disabled delegates and other individuals from around the world converged on this city for INDEPENDENCE 92... The World Congress on Disability. Along with a huge display-type technology exposition, over 100 workshops and plenary sessions, international craft displays and cultural music/drama/literary entertainment, this was a phenomenal event held in the Vancouver Trade and Convention Centre.

Rick Hansen, from "Man in Motion Tour," was the conference chairperson. He spoke briefly at the opening and closing ceremonies, as well as at the gala banquet.

The theme of the conference was independence, and buzz words such as empowerment, consumer control, equality and self-determination flowed freely in the sessions and over coffee.

One almost didn't feel disabled in the atmosphere of the convention centre. After all, "handicap" is merely a label and as one person so aptly put it, labels are for jars, not people. For a few days, we, as disabled persons, were the majority.

Packed-to-the-doors workshops such as Disability and Sexuality, Empowerment Through Individual Funding, Independent Living Examples and Access Through Housing, Community, Transportation and Tourism illustrated the goals, aspirations and dreams of those in attendance.

Many workshops were so popular people were turned away.

The technology exposition displayed a fully accessible house built on site by Canada Mortgage and Housing Corporation. Also, a prototype of a wheelchair-lift equipped motor coach was parked on "Independence Street," a fabricated "city" street with a school, bank, park and restaurant, laid out in the Exposition Hall. The bus was a dream. It had a fully wheelchair accessible bathroom along with ample maneuvering space for large wheelchairs. In talking to the company representative, we learned that Saskatchewan is the only province with legislation allowing this length of bus (five feet longer than usual) on the road. Saskatchewan Transportation Company (STC) is currently considering the purchase of at least one such bus. More power to them!

The Neil Squire Foundation had a fully automated work station set up in the CIBC bank on Independence Street, complete with computer and robotic arm.

It was enlightening to meet disabled persons from Russia, Zimbabwe and Haiti, as well as England, Australia and a host of other countries. One fellow from Moscow, Yuri Kiselev, came to the conference with only the clothes on his back, scooting around on a wooden board with four wheels. That was his mode of transportation. Coming from a politically bankrupt nation,

Yuri stated that in his country, "invalids," as disabled persons are called, have no rights, even to medical care. And recent political reform in Russia has done little to better this, except that disabled persons are now allowed to be seen in public. At the closing banquet, he was presented with a wheelchair by the organization that sponsored his attending the conference.

One could only imagine the culture shock for persons from the Third World to attend a conference such as this in a country such as ours. This disparity created two trains of thought in the minds of many delegates. The first was gratitude for what we do have in the industrialized world to provide independence for persons with disabilities. The second, and probably most prominent, was to acknowledge how very far we have to go to realize the goal of true independent living.

It was enlightening to find out what other countries and even what other parts of our country have done to empower or disempower the lives of people with disabilities. A representative from Alberta stated that Alberta funds $27 million a year for their social assistance attendant service program.

In the attendant services workshop, Brian Cruikshank, author of 'Attendant Services in Canada,' stated that Saskatchewan is considered the worst province for providing attendant services.

On the bright side, a new fully accessible housing co-operative is now established in Vancouver, the Stanley Noble Stronge Complex. Its barrier-free apartments are almost fully controlled by a high-tech environmental control unit (ECU) attached to your wheelchair. The elevator is also controlled by the ECU, allowing you to choose from your wheelchair which floor you desire. This is brand new technology.

Conversely, it was amazing to hear that Japan, which is progressive in many technological advances, is just beginning to see the need for disability awareness and physical/psychological accessibility in their cities.

To capture the essence of a conference like INDEPEN-DENCE '92 is practically impossible. It was an experience not soon rivaled and not easily duplicated.

Vancouver was a wonderful host city. Its accessibility (structurally, in transportation as well as in attitude) was commendable. It was good to be able to travel on virtually any mode of local transportation from taxis to city buses to the Sky Train and ferry shuttles.

Sitting in a common area with dozens of persons with wheelchairs, canes, crutches, guide dogs, hearing devices and scooters, along with those having less visible disabilities, made one thing quite evident: we are not alone in our quest for empowerment. Other people have achieved it, are achieving it or have a dream to achieve it. Thirty years ago, a conference such as this was inconceivable, much less the radical concepts that stand behind it.

Empowerment was the benchmark phrase throughout the conference. One workshop outlined that there were two levels of empowerment: individual self-determination (including the right to take risks and be in control of our lives) and collective empowerment (on boards, committees and with government).

Rachel Hurst, from a disabled women's movement in England, stated during the opening session: "The time has come for governments and others to stop TALKING about the need for change and start ACTING upon it." We are used to asking others to provide services for us but now we are beginning to step forth and create our own way. Consumer control... no longer are we merely asking for help, but advocating on our own behalf.

A woman from Spanish-speaking Curacao stated that "disabled persons should be recognized as citizens and extended the *rights afforded to all citizens," such as the right to choose where to live.*

In the workshop, "Participation: Fact or Fiction," it was stated that many disabled persons have passed through different stages... from being ignored or, at best, relegated to being "cared for" paternalistically or as charity cases. We are progressing from isolation to hope to solidarity to independence and equality. But we have a long way to go. When we are not given the opportunity to participate in society, the workshop speakers stated that we are filled with a sense of powerlessness, that our opinion doesn't matter. It does.

Joshua Malinga from Zimbabwe quoted the Bible, "Without a vision, the people perish."

Winston Churchill was also quoted, "Never surrender. Never. Never."

As these comments ring in our ears, let's allow the following poem, also quoted at the conference, to empower us to"fly."

> *When I was about to fly they said, "Oh, you can't fly."*
> *When I was about to sing they said, "Oh, you can't sing."*
> *I decided not to listen to the bores*
> *because how can those who have never been*
> *"about to" understand*
> *that **even birds with broken wings... have wings.***

Here's to the future!

■ ■ ■

Bernice and I communicated often by telephone between Birch Hills and Regina, sharing news and needs. Hearing her voice, bright and cheerful, lifted my heart and energized me for the day's duties.

One day in April, 1993, she called with sad news. Connie's father, Stan Oxelgren, had suddenly passed away. "Pray for Connie and her family, Mom. They need strength and guidance these days. Her dad has been her encourager and support, physically and spiritually. It will be difficult for them all."

Carol, sister Lisa and other family members rallied to support Connie and one another. The promises of God became a foundation for their daily walk. "Fear thou not; for I am with thee: be not dismayed; for I am thy God: I will strengthen thee; yea, I will help thee; I will uphold thee" (Isa. 41:10).

In October that same year, we lost my sister Nina to cancer. Though unable to attend the funeral, Bernice prayed for Uncle Ted and all of us as we said good-bye to a dear aunt. We miss her presence among us, cheerful, generous and kind.

The flesh is not only weak, but so perishable. "All flesh is as grass, and all the glory of man as the flower of grass. The grass withereth, and the flower thereof falleth away" (1 Peter 1:24). But thanks be to God for in His eternal purpose, the spirit lives to inherit His promises. "Eye has not seen, nor ear heard, neither have entered into the heart of man, the things which God hath prepared for them that love Him" (1 Cor. 2:9).

Bernice struggled periodically with feelings of inferiority and timidity. She fought back with the sword of the Spirit... "I can do all things through Christ who strengthens me" (Phil. 4:13). She remembered God's exhortation to a fearful Moses to use the rod in his hand.

Use now what God has given you,
Count not its worth as small;

> *God does not ask great things of you,*
> *Just faithfulness, that's all.*
>
> —Anon

■ ■ ■

Many opportunities to "do" and "be" presented themselves at Wascana. It was too exciting and challenging to resist.

Jil mastered mouth painting in her watercolour and pottery classes. Seeing Jil at work motivated Bernice to try her own skills. She used her hands, holding her project up close as instructors moved from student to student, offering help when needed. For starters, Bernice painted Christmas cards for aunts and uncles, a restful winter scene. She tackled larger pieces too, one a farm scene for me, and another colourful abstract creation, which allowed her to be more free and reckless. Examples of her pottery can be seen in relatives' homes. My cherished piece is a manger scene featuring Mary, Joseph and baby Jesus, with a shepherd boy and lamb. I can visualize her labour of love over that figurine, thanking God with every brush stroke that He came to us in Jesus to offer forgiveness and hope.

Bernice discovered the Christian Prairie Writer's Guild in Regina. Again, lights came on in her mind. *Just what I was looking for,* she thought. Through this group she met several Saskatchewan writers and became involved in the publication of their magazine, *Panorama*, occasionally contributing an article.

Further in the inspirational line, she heard that the Christian writer's workshop "God Uses Ink" would be held at Caronport, Saskatchewan. She attended in May, 1993, and May, 1995, arranging the trip by herself, including a caregiver to accompany her. The 1993 instructor was Lorna Dueck, who became a friend and encourager. Phil Callaway taught the 1995 seminar, sharing much good-natured counsel.

Late in 1993, Bernice involved herself in a hands-on outreach program in her church. Being one of its many singles, she initiated a monthly social evening for single moms and other singles. She had a dream of organizing a babysitting service, but doing all the planning by phone from a wheelchair had its drawbacks. She valued the opportunity to fellowship with other singles.

Closer to home at WRC, she knew several residents who would appreciate having a Bible study, so she received permission to conduct a half-hour study in the games room. She placed posters in strategic places:

DOES GOD KNOW I'M HERE?
DOES HE CARE?

- **Is there more to life than mere existence—trying to make the best of it?**
- **Does God have a blueprint, a purpose for our lives?**
- **Is God watching us only "from a distance"—or can we have a close personal relationship with Him?**

These questions and more will be discussed at an informal Interdenominational Coffee Bible Study held in the Main 5 Games Room every Tuesday, 6:30 p.m.
Residents, family and staff welcome!

"For I know the plans I have for you, declares the Lord, plans to prosper you and not to harm you, plans to give you hope and a future" (Jer. 29:11, NIV).

For more info., contact Bernice Boyes —529

On Tuesdays, she was happy to see Randy, Joan, Harold, Esther, Joe, Jim, Norman and occasionally others. The time had to be changed due to preparations for bed and other unavoidable things, but on the whole these were the regulars. Sometimes Bernice invited a friend to sing or relate a story. These informal little studies, with shared prayer requests, continued each week until three days before she died. Incredible.

Bernice participated enthusiastically in WRC programs for the betterment of daily resident living. She joined Jil, Connie and Sherry in their efforts on the Residents' Council. She offered her services to the South Saskatchewan Independent Living Centre (SSILC) where Sherry shone like a beacon. Extending from there, like helping hands, committees and sub-committees searched out every possible (and sometimes impossible) way that life could be improved for the disabled. Bernice wanted to champion them all.

Scanning this list of activities, it's a wonder she had the time and strength. Somewhere along the way she undertook to be a telephone counselor for 100 Huntley Street, one day a week for six months. What a new and challenging experience. She confessed to being thrown off guard one day when someone called to ask advice regarding his homosexual tendencies. She referred him to a pastor.

Her family and friends had learned not to be too surprised when a new project appeared on Bernice's agenda, but when, early in 1995, she became an Avon distributor, we were appalled.

"Bernice! This is too much. You'll wear yourself out!"

"It's not that hard, Mom. I have a captive clientele here, in staff and residents. It's good business training for me."

We were not convinced that her business acumen could be improved by selling cosmetics. In fact, we agreed with the comment of a casual observer who watched Jil and Bernice organize the fall craft sale: "These girls have executive ability. From their wheelchairs, aided by computer and telephone, they plan to the last detail, a massive two-day event, supported by a small platoon of volunteers."

Chapter Ten

The YWAM Adventure

One of the Main 5 nurses, Debbie, planned to attend the Youth With a Mission Discipleship Training School (DTS) in Salem, Oregon, in the fall of 1993. Her enthusiasm lit a fire under Bernice. *Dare I even think about this?* Debbie offered to be her caregiver. That did it. But when they shared this great idea with me, they met a long face and cold water.

What accommodation do they have for the disabled? Is it accessible and safe for a wheelchair? What about toilet and bathing facilities? So far away... in the winter? How can you be ready so quickly? What about health insurance? Bernice looked at me and burst into tears. *Dear Lord, have I no faith or vision?* Sorry, Bernice, we'll think and pray about it.

There would be another opportunity in March, next year. In the intervening months, she contacted the YWAM director and formally applied to come. Accommodation and accessibility were checked out. She found excellent health insurance coverage. The computer would accompany her. The *new* computer and printer. I related to Elisha's friend in the Old Testament who lost his axe head in the water: "Alas, master, for it was borrowed." But, as we read, Elisha intervened and the iron swam. We insured the computer, and it made the trip without a scratch. Can prudence and faith walk hand in hand? My daughter taught me how to combine wisdom and wonder. Always leave room for God to surprise you. Her prayers and persuasive communications won me over. Not that I could have stopped her, had it come to a battle of wills, or would have wanted to, in that case.

Dear Mom,

Neat print on my new computer printer, eh??!! I just finished talking to you on the phone (about the tapes you want to give away, etc.) and I felt like I should write you a note to talk to you further about YWAM. Yes, THAT subject.

I really want you to feel secure about my going. Your opinion and approval means a lot to me; but my goals and vision mean a lot to me, too. I would not want to be torn between your approval and my goals. Mothers are notorious for not wanting their "little girls" to go even one step out of the comfort zone. That's understandable and I love you for it. That shows how much you care about me. And you rate in the "above average" level when it comes to love and care. I could never ask for a better mother and friend.

The ultimate test in trusting God for the safety of your children is to let them go, let them break new ground... ride the bike without training wheels. The first step for you and Dad was letting me go to school, then spend the night away from home. Next big step was when I moved away from home to Saskatoon; to a safe environment, but not under your immediate care. Independence took a step back as I returned home for a year, making my move to Regina that much of a bigger step for me and for you than it would have been had I gone directly from Saskatoon.

Now, the next step is a doozy, but I have been exercising my wings of independence over the years and feel it is time to truly test them. How will I ever know if it can be done if I don't try? Life is all about taking calculated chances. You conquered barriers to attend Bible college and go to the mission field. My barriers are different but I have missionary blood in me. I come by it naturally to want to serve my Lord with the gifts He has given me. YWAM gives me the opportunity to take training at a size I can handle—no long, drawn-out degree courses to zap my time and energy for years. It's probably the closest thing I'll get to the mission field, so much a part of my heritage and now an attainable goal for the first time for me. And their zeal for God at YWAM really inspires me. I have felt closer to the Lord since this YWAM thing began than I have since Seeker days. And the maturity of the decade that has elapsed since then deepens that hunger and thirst for righteousness. I have learned a lot over the past few years especially; about myself, the world and my relationship with my Creator. Granted, there have been spiritually lean times often, too. But I never lost the sense of Jesus working in my life. The winter of my soul (a season which has its place in the scheme of things—and which has its own moments of beauty) is for me turning to spring and I am excited about my future.

In reading Loren Cunningham's book about how YWAM started (you read it, too), I realized many things about guidance. One is that we can't let our personal feelings get in the way of hearing God's voice. That's advice for both of us. Neither of us can pray, "Oh, Lord, I know You see things my way, so knock her over the head so she will see it as it really is."

Contrary to how I might sound in my enthusiasm, I am careful to be open to God's will if it is to stay here. I am aware of the danger of letting the glitter of the trip blind my judgement, and I am determined NOT to let that happen. I want God's will above all else in my life, and I think I have learned a lot from the false start of a few months ago regarding going in January. I will take it slowly, one step at a time, so I don't make any wrong moves.

I know your heart. Even if God were to hit you with a light-ning bolt saying, "Bernice is supposed to go!"—you would still have reservations. But could you honestly stand in the way of God's best for my life after having such a clear indication? In His still small voice, God IS trying to speak to you and to me, telling us what He wants. Let's neither of us make Him resort to lightning bolts to get through to us.

Sure, there will be unforeseen hurdles to overcome when I get there, as well as before I leave. Although one thing about hav-ing known Connie is that I've learned how to cover most bases. Her travel plan is incredible! The neat thing about being in the will of God is that we know He will look after the hurdles... maybe not always in a way we thought, but always in the best way. Part of faith is trusting God for the things we cannot see. Don't worry, though. I plan on covering all the areas I can pos-sibly think of.

My times are in His hands. The safest place to be, whether in Oregon or in Regina.

I love you, Mom.

Your daughter,
Bernice

P.S. In case you noticed, yes, I am, for now planning on going. "I, being in the way, the Lord led me...." Remember that quote?! You taught me well! I will walk in that direction and trust Jesus to guide my steps, WHATEVER way that ends up being.

The steps of a good man are ordered by the Lord:
and he delighteth in His way. Though he fall,
he shall not be utterly cast down:
for the Lord upholdeth him with His hand.

—*Psalm 37:23-24*

January 31, 1994

Expect great things from God;
attempt great things for God. —William Carey

"Dear friends,

"Very belated Christmas greetings to you! Please forgive me for not writing at Christmas, I was holding off for this very special letter I knew I'd be sending in January. May 1994 be rich in God's revelation of Himself to your heart.

"'*For I know the plans I have for you, declares the Lord, plans to prosper you and not to harm you, plans to give you hope and a future' (Jer. 29:11, NIV).*

"Two very important (and exciting!) things have happened to me over the past while. I'd like to share them with you. First, I've recently been looking for government funding sources to purchase some needed computer equipment, and God has wonderfully supplied funds for that through the Department of Education's Vocational Rehabilitation for Disabled Persons program. I sincerely praise the Lord for continually meeting my needs! The computer has helped tremendously with doing my children's book... I continue to seek the right publisher. I can fully trust that God's timing is impeccable. (By the way, this letter is being typed on my new system, which I plan to take with me. Where? you ask. Read on....)

"Secondly, (are you sitting down??) I have mentioned to a few of my friends how I've been feeling that some kind of change is coming to my life. Well, the Lord is opening the way for me to attend a Youth With a Mission (YWAM) Discipleship Training School starting March 21, 1994. It would be held at the mission base in Salem, Oregon, and would extend to August 13, if I stay for both the training *and* outreach period. It is a great opportunity for me to grow in the Lord in a Christ-centered, well-established and highly recommended training centre; and to fulfill a lifelong dream of being in a missions environment. Debbie, a friend of mine who has been a nurse on my ward at Wascana for several years, is already in Salem to take a course (with the goal of full-time work with YWAM). She has generously offered to stay on and help with my personal care while I am there. What a blessing THAT is. An added blessing is that since she is going first, she will be able to "case the joint" and see what I'll need when I come. I initially chose Salem because that was where Debbie is going, but as time progressed and I had contact with them, I really sensed God had a purpose for directing me to that particular base. The school director's wife is a nurse, which is an extra assurance of support.

"I have thought and prayed much about this decision; I am more than aware of the step of faith this is for me with my level of disability, and it will be a challenge at times, but if my heavenly Father is in something, the boundaries are endless because His strength is infinite! I can choose to merely live life or to *LIVE*, even if that means taking some calculated risks. To become a part of something bigger than myself, to catch God's vision for the world beyond my little sphere of influence, that has been my desire. Chalk it up to my missionary family heritage, I guess! God Himself only knows where this will lead me, but I need to be obedient in this next step. One step (wheel) at a time!

"The mission base is basically accessible to a wheelchair and they have a specially adapted dorm room with private bathroom. They are more than willing to work around my physical limitations in living and working. In fact, they were quite excited to have me come. And they could really utilize my writing skills in their publications department while I'm there. Great opportunity for training in professional writing for me.

"Usually, students take the training session and then go out on an outreach ministry to Europe, third world countries or parts of the States for the last two months of the program, but instead, I *might* stay at the base to work in the area of writing. I'm not sure how the Lord is leading me regarding that yet.

"Like I said, this is a real humdinger of a faith-move for me and a lot of things need to be worked out before I leave. But my entire life has been a lesson in the fact that nothing is impossible with God. And the Lord is already opening the way for some of my concerns to be met, such as holding my bed at Wascana while I'm gone, as well as my success in finding a comprehensive medical insurance that will cover disability-related medical expenses. I'd very much appreciate your prayers as I prepare to go, set up my finances, etc., and of course, during my training period as well. Any questions or prayer needs of your own? Feel free to call or write. I'll keep in touch."

Because He lives,
Bernice Boyes

■ ■ ■

In Bernice's absence, her Wascana room would be occupied by a respite patient. All her belongings had to be removed, so Uncle Jim offered their basement as temporary storage space. My friend Adeline helped me load and unload several times. Foam mattresses, pillows, bedding, toilet seat and guard rail had to travel with Bernice.

The big departure day arrived. Two wheelchairs were secured and readied for travel. Darlene Miller was her travelling companion. Bernice, wedged into the narrow on-board wheelchair, was radiant with excitement. Well-wishers Tim and Darlene, Ernie, Connie, Aunts Anna, Dorothy and Margaret, Uncles John and Jim, and Adeline joined me in surrounding her with tender ministrations. Then she was off on silver wings and our prayers.

Now convinced that God could care for her as He promised, I let her go with peace in my heart. She was following her dream.

She kept me informed by telephone... easier than writing letters. The room she shared with Debbie couldn't be better, she reported. "Large and comfortable. Our own toilet and bath. Accessible to dining and lounge areas." I could feel her happiness.

Most exciting, of course, were the study sessions. Missionaries and Bible teachers shared their wisdom and experience, among them George Dawidiuk, Winkie Pratney, Dan Sherman and John Bills. "Grandma" Agnes Wolfe, the cook, and her family became fast friends.

John Bills, a man of compassion for the down and out, sponsored a week of outreach to Portland's inner city. The students planned to live in a church basement, cook their own meals and spend afternoons and evenings on the streets. They sang, shared their faith and talked to anyone who would listen. Bernice's impressions:

"That week in Portland was one of the highlights of the DTS for me, partly because it was the closest I will get to an outreach experience with the students. It opened my eyes to another world that exists all around us, where people are homeless, sick, starving and hopeless. For the first time I saw someone sleeping on the street. I admit to being a little fearful. John Bills has a servant heart. He seems comfortable with me, perhaps because he has seen so much of problems and distress. His daily talks with us challenge my level of compassion. It's easy to be gracious at a distance."

The students brought a bed and mattress for Bernice, and they carried her wheelchair whenever they met with inaccessibility. I was unaware of this expedition until later. God applied my prayers to "wherever most needed."

Among Bernice's mementos from YWAM were bundles of loving notes from the hospitality department, faxes from WRC and the Harvest City Church, a long encouraging letter from cousin Wes, and many communications from me. For Bernice's birthday, April 15, Connie sent a card featuring an accessible toilet, complete with grab bar and thirty audible flushes!

YWAM—April 28, 1994
7085 Battlecreek Rd. NE, Salem, Oregon 97301

"Hi from the wet state!

"We are having a blast here in Oregon. The weather is very often rainy although we've had a couple of warm spells in April where I actually got a sunburn on my face!

"**Question of the day**: Do you know what an Oregonian car pool is? **Answer**: A convertible with the top down! No exaggeration some days, it seems!

"I'm getting along well... almost everything is very accessible for me, and people are great about helping me. I'm making new friends and learning a lot about myself and my relationship with the Lord in prayer and as a daughter of my heavenly Father. I'm also using my computer quite a bit for my assignments and doing some work for the staff (mainly setting up files for the kitchen, typing newsletters and doing some water well usage charts). It's four miles to Salem from our base... too far and too hilly for me to walk, but I have hopped in a car a few times to go out for coffee. We were at a European café last week... wonderful cheesecake! Cappuccino and latté (cappuccino, steamed milk and flavouring) coffee is big here. We are an hour from the ocean, the mountains and Silver Creek Falls (a popular tourist area). Last weekend some of us went to the coast... just for a drive since it was a bit rainy. Beautiful scenery! It's so nice and green here. Tall evergreens and hills everywhere. Tulips and daffodils blooming, plus some fruit trees. Moss growing even on some sidewalks because of all the rain.

"With 80 people on staff and all the students, it is a very international place. There are Americans, a couple from Switzerland, a lady from Russia (Olga, who is becoming a good friend), and a guy from Canada (Mike from BC: he recently gave his heart to the Lord after being a gang member and drug pusher! Quite a story. He's like a big teddy bear now!). The head of the kitchen (we call her "Grandma") is originally from Saskatchewan. She and her family are on their way to India in June. Slavic ministries are particularly big. There are several people from Latin America, too. One morning we sang, "God Is So Good" in whatever language we speak. It was neat!

"TIDBITS: For my birthday, my friends had a cake and they decorated my wheelchair with streamers and balloons (which I had to wear all day!). We went out for coffee into Salem, too. Neat friends. We went to a Phil Driscoll concert last Sunday at a local church. It was VERY good. Right now, there is a writer's school going on for two weeks. I hope to talk to their speakers about my writing, even though I don't have time, because of the DTS, to take the writer's course. One of the writers used to work as a health nurse in Birch Hills for a short time! Talk about small world!"

A Day in the Life

- classes begin at 8 a.m. (Except Monday and Tuesday when the entire base meets for worship and prayer. Great times, learning to discern the clear direction of God as we pray about a situation and sing powerful new choruses.)
- each week we have a new speaker who lectures from 10 a.m. to noon. So far, topics have included prayer, lifestyle issues, relationships and Sonship (seeing God, not as an authoritarian or a distant deity, but as my Abba Father or 'Daddy').

- the afternoon is spent doing work duties, mine on the computer.
- the evenings are for homework and getting to know each other. Relationships among the students and staff are very important here.
- occasionally we go into Salem or Portland to minister with a street team or youth group. Haven't done that much yet.
- the base has a bookstore where we visit or drink coffee.
- Friday night there is a service here which the community comes to. The speaker we have had all week usually speaks.

"Debbie, my friend who is helping me, is doing fine. I really appreciate her help and friendship. She plans on staying with YWAM, maybe using her nursing skills on one of their mercy ships. I am waiting to see how God directs *me* after the school. One thing I am seeing here for sure is that He DOES lead specifically in our lives, if we seek Him. 'I (God) WILL be found of him' who 'seeks Me with all his heart...'

"How are *you* doing? Please *write* and keep me informed in your lives. Sorry for not writing to you personally."

Bernice

■ ■ ■

Early in July, just past the mid-point of the session, Bernice and Debbie found it necessary to come back to Regina to treat a pressure sore. Bernice spoke with exaggerated calm on the phone.

"It's okay, Mom. Nothing serious at all. Just a couple of weeks and it will be healed over."

We met them at the airport, stuff and all. Well, not quite all.

"Where's the computer?"

"Actually, Mom, I didn't bring it because I'm going back to finish up."

"Bernice!" Stunned and speechless, I couldn't think of anything to say.

"Mom, I do want to finish what I started. It's so exciting and interesting. The only problem is that Debbie won't be able to go back. However, I will find someone else. I have assurance from the Lord on that."

I continued being stunned and speechless. I had learned by now not to react hastily.

Bernice had alerted Main 5 of her imminent return. The respite patient was transferred elsewhere and we found enough bedding and other necessities for the night.

The next day we brought from Browns only what would be needed for the two weeks of recovery. In the meantime, Bernice busied herself with homework and compiled a mailing list. She talked to friends at church about her need for a caregiver. Sure enough, according to her assurance from the Lord, Julie Harrison came along.

Julie had been hoping and praying for an opportunity to attend one of the Discipleship Training Seminars (DTS) at YWAM. Perfect. Thank You, Lord. She came to Main 5 to acquaint herself with the details of the care needed. Bernice made all the arrangements for their return trip. I could only shake my head in amazement. Just a little over schedule, they were off, on wings and prayers again. *Guardian angel, ride with them.*

Word from Oregon in the following weeks accentuated the positive in every way.

"I haven't had a cold all summer, Mom! I eat well and sleep well. Julie is having fun. She's taking courses with me. We've been to the beach. Now I can say I've waded in both oceans, east and west. We're learning a lot. There's a real missionary spirit here. Some of the students have already been to other countries. I wish there was something I could do to help others. I'm praying about it."

Bernice's friend Patricia Cook, a Regina writer, interviewed Bernice regarding her trip to Oregon. Her article appeared in the fall 1994 edition of *Panorama*, a publication of Christian writers in the city. Designing the layout for the fall edition of *Panorama* was part of Bernice's homework during her "sick leave" time back in Regina. To quote Bernice's words from Patricia's article: "It was a vision-building time for me to see what God could do with my life when I was willing to step out in faith. I needed to focus on solutions rather than problems and not let my fears, or the fears of others, get in the way of what God wanted me to do. As Lynn Johnson says in her comic strip, *For Better or Worse*, 'Where there's a wheel, there's a way!'"

Late in August, the two travellers returned, tired but enthused, followed by luggage, boxes, bundles and wheelchairs.

Making up for lost time with Connie had become urgent, for she would soon leave to pursue studies at Carleton University in Ottawa. This move had been on her mind for a long time. Carleton offered accommodation and care for students with disabilities; the care being provided by students who signed up for this duty. The provision of this unique symbiotic arrangement strongly motivated Connie to choose Carleton.

The prospect of being separated for years perhaps, except for short visits, weighed on their hearts. But Connie felt compelled to grasp this opportunity to further her life work. Bernice, for her part, had plans that would take her on a parallel track toward her own future. They vowed to keep in touch by telephone and fax, pledging to pray for each other.

We missed Connie's appearance at the door, the coffee breaks in the cafeteria, the shopping trips to the mall. Before long, however, Jil came along with plans for the craft sale in November. Life must go on.

The Craft Sale

The WRC Extended Care Resident's Council serves as an auxiliary aid to fund and promote helpful devices to make life easier for residents. For instance, a simple attachment is available which enables the resident to operate the telephone, TV or radio by blowing through a straw. There are state-of-the-art environmental control units (ENCO) designed for persons living independently which will, on command, regulate every mechanical and electronic device in a room or house. Modified versions of this type of unit are used by some WRC residents.

Jil and her fellow planners, always on the lookout for ways to raise funds, came up with the idea of a craft sale. They called it Crafty Creations. The large concourse at WRC seemed an ideal location, and so, in late November, 1994, Crafty Creations was launched. A massive telephone campaign alerted crafters, and response exceeded expectations. Bernice, in charge of promotion and advertising, set herself to contact all news media and prepare posters. I went with her to a television show where she displayed a few crafts and chatted with the amiable host.

Forty-two crafters signed up. Jack Harker and his volunteers arranged to borrow or rent tables. Housekeeping provided sheets to cover them. Jil and her mother pored over diagrams and lists like generals planning a military campaign. The refreshment centre served up cookies, muffins, cinnamon buns and coffee. Jack staffed the kitchen, turning out countless pans of goodies. Visitors followed the aroma of fresh baking to his corner.

Crafters, mainly from the Regina and Moose Jaw areas, presented a colourful display of unique creations, a tribute to the fertile imaginations of our citizens. Crafty Creations closed Saturday afternoon with everyone feeling satisfied the job had been well done.

CHAPTER ELEVEN

A Valley Experience

When the DTS classes closed in August, the students had plans for practical, hands-on work in some missions capacity. A few went abroad to continue previous work. Others had plans for pioneer work in Mexico, the States or Canada. Bernice, unable to undertake such strenuous projects, offered to organize and mail the Wolfe's newsletter when they reached India, their field of service. Agnes would work in a clinic, while Nathanael would home-school the three children and supervise the household. We admired their dedication and prayed for God's protection.

Bernice found a few labour-saving devices to aid her in the printing and mailing of dozens of letters. Agnes sent her handwritten letters, and Bernice typed and photocopied them. Envelopes were addressed and mailed. Eventually she graduated to address labels, but folding and envelope-stuffing needed hands. I was able to help now and then.

Sensing a blue mood behind her ready smile, I reminded her that the Lord had allowed her to use her particular gifts to meet a definite need. "Remember that saying?" I asked. "'God does not ask great things of you, just faithfulness, that's all.'" The prophet Micah observed that devotion rates higher than performance: "He hath shewed thee, O man, what is good; and what doth the Lord require of thee, but to do justly, to love mercy, and to walk humbly with thy God?" (Micah 6:8).

After the emotional and spiritual high of the trip to Oregon, Bernice experienced a sense of anticlimax. She missed the good times. She envied, a little, those who had embarked on exciting endeavours for the Lord. During the winter of 1994-95, she set out again to revive her work on the children's book. The autobiography, long dormant, had fresh insight and experience to add new life to its pages. Repeated rejections by editors had almost discouraged her from trying again. The new computer spurred her on, but that surge of new enthusiasm soon flagged. The task was too demanding for the available strength.

■ ■ ■

Her journal, about that time, revealed an intimate conversation she had with her Lord and Saviour, drawing comfort and strength from Him.

Dear Bernice:

There is something I would like to say to you that I really think you need to hear. You are a very special person. **My daughter.** *And I want you to know that I love you. You don't have to perform to gain My approval (or anybody else's). Even if you only get to play the part of the tree shrub in your school* *play. Even if you forget your one line on opening night. You are still My child and I am **proud** of you.*

I hold you in My arms. It's a safe place to be. No matter how many slings and arrows of outrageous fortune are hurled at you, I will be your shelter. Your faith in Me will be your shield. I believe in you and your potential. Even if you have a hard time believing in yourself right now, allow Me to instill in you true confidence; not because of what you can do, but because of who you are. A daughter of the King of kings.

You have special abilities, personality traits and attributes that no one else has. You have a purpose to fulfill that no one else on the face of the earth can accomplish in the same way or with the same effectiveness. I knew you before you were conceived. I had a plan for you. Before the world was formed, I knew Bernice Boyes would exist, that you would come to know Me and love Me and serve Me. You are not a product of chance nor is the direction of your life left to happenstance. I am with you every single step of the way.

Remember to watch for pridefulness, however. True humility is meekness, not weakness. It is knowing wherein your strength lies.

*I root for your ultimate happiness, My dear, sweet daughter. Don't think of Me as Someone who sits up in heaven trying to think of ways to make your life difficult. I am your **Daddy**. My Father-heart aches to hold you in My care, but you often stay at arm's length just when you need My comfort the most. Allow Me to melt that self-sufficiency with the warmth of My Spirit. Run to My arms when you skin your knee. Let Me rub the balm of Gilead on your wounded soul. You are not inferior, My daughter. You are a diamond of grace.*

Love, your Daddy
Jehovah-Abba

Jesus, Saviour, Lord to me
My hope, my trust is in You;
When my world is in turmoil,
My soul need not be.
By faith I stand on Your promises,
Sit at Your feet,
Kneel in Your presence,
Rest in Your love.
As I walk on the road toward eternity,
Help me to keep my eyes fixed on You, Jesus,
The author and perfecter of my faith.
Though Satan may hurl darts at me
From every side... taunting, jeering,
Tempting, alluring, trying to deceive,
Whispering negative thoughts in my ear.
Jesus, I choose to walk on, eyes front,
My mission ever before me.
A servant of Jesus,
Dead to sin but alive to God.
Prescribe to me glasses, Lord,
That see others only through eyes
Of agape love.
Your perspective, not mine.
May I be near sighted
When it comes to the faults of others;
Clear sighted when dealing with my own sin,
Above all, Jesus, I want You to know
That I trust You with my life.
Thank You for being there for me.

Ever and always,
Your child, Bernice

Fill my cup again, Lord,
As I lift it up to You,
I see how empty I have let my vessel become.
When I first knew You,
I was constantly kneeling under the tap of Your Spirit,
laughing with delight
as the Water of life not only filled, but lavishly gushed
over the brim of my vessel, splashing
refreshingly over my entire being...
I couldn't drink it in fast enough.
That was my first love.

I don't know when it began changing...
but one day I realized my Water tasted a bit stale. Strange.
My cup needed a refill but I didn't have time
to keep trekking to the Fountain...
"Maybe I'll just drink bottled water for a while," I thought.
"Think of all the time I'll save when I don't have to keep running
to the Source.
Water is water, after all, right?"

Wrong. (Like the frog who slowly boiled to death
because he didn't realize the water he was soaking in
was gradually heating up) I was slipping slowly,
almost imperceptively into a spiritually life-threatening state.

Oh, maybe I was successful in what I was doing.
I may have even accomplished things for the Kingdom of God,
But inside me something had changed.
The stream of living Water that I no longer sought
virtually dried up.
And with it, so did my soul,

because although the never-changing Source of the stream
is God's Spirit,
the funnel He pours through is my spirit.
As my demand for the Water gradually ebbed away,
and my funnel clogged with earthly cholesterol,
To the same degree, the intensity of the flow also ebbed away...
So by choosing the "bottled water" of superficial mediocrity
over the fresh Water of vital Christianity,
I dehydrated my soul from within.
Funny how long it took for me to realize this.
I guess the "bottled water" took the edge of my thirst away
So I didn't realize how needy I really was.

Like the person driving along the highway who suddenly realizes
with a frightening realization that he had fallen asleep at the
wheel. In a few short seconds, the car has veered dangerously off
course... and if not immediately righted could end disastrously...

Lord, refill my cup with the fresh water of Your Spirit...
Cleanse out the hard water deposits that have been left
in my heart...
May my earthen vessel be emptied of me
And filled with You.
"That the excellency of the power may be of God and not of us."

Lord, refill my cup.
I'm thirsty for You.

—Bernice Boyes, 1994

Bernice wrote the following article for *Panorama* in the spring of 1995.

From the Skin Out
(Is what you see what you get?)

I am not disabled. If you look at a picture of me in my wheelchair, you might want to question the truthfulness of that statement, but let me explain.

Most of us want to be accepted for who we are and what we can contribute to society. How short we are, how tall, how thin, how stout, how beautiful, how plain... that is only us from the skin out, and we don't want to be judged by such factors. We can be 4 foot 8, scrawny, with a big nose and two left feet but have a "heart" the size of Texas.

So then, if we look beyond appearances, I am not disabled. My body happens to be but I am not. Does this change how we view a person with a disability when we meet them? I think it should.

Take Stephen Hawking. He is so severely physically disabled that he cannot do anything for himself, and he is able to speak only by a computer synthesized voice. If you met him in his home, your first impression would be that he is incapable of anything resembling a life. Yet he has written several scholarly books, has a doctorate in physics and continues to lecture at prestigious universities by his computer voice. Conclusion: there is life after disability.

Our high-tech world has made it possible for persons with very significant disabilities, such as those who breathe with the help of mechanical respirators, to be out of bed, to work and to live in their own apartments. Technology has opened the world to them. Using various methods to access the computer system (from mini keyboards to mouth sticks to voice-control), they can run their household, get university degrees, do research, write books, even give lectures from their bed or wheelchair. The options are limitless. No, I take that back. The options are limited, but by two basic barriers: attitudes (my own as well as those of others) and availability of finances.

Over the years, I've seen a variety of reactions to my disability, ranging from the bizarre to the disappointing. There was the boy who actually thought I was someone's *science project* when he saw my friend pushing me in my wheelchair one day. He'd obviously not seen anything quite like me before! Then there were those who told me not to bother completing high school because it would be too difficult for me to handle the work. You can guess how I responded to that suggestion!

Since then, I have started a career in writing, been on a Christian mission trip, participated in disability research and government negotiations. I don't plan to spend my time merely filling my days playing bingo or watching talk shows as some might expect. Life has all kinds of potential!

My disability is not the worst thing that could happen to me. I know people who have no physical needs to speak of, but are severely "handicapped" because of the troubles they've experienced in life and how they've chosen to handle them. We all have challenges, strength and weaknesses. I can help you with yours and you can help me with mine.

Everyone has a disablement of some kind... physical, emotional or spiritual. I believe handicaps of the soul are infinitely more intense than any physical disability. And healing of our souls through the forgiving love of Jesus is infinitely more critical than physical healing.

As a Christian, I am assured that God sees the real 'me' even if no one else does. *"Man looks at the outward appearance, but the Lord looks at the heart"* (1 Sam. 16:7, NIV). My personal relationship with the Creator of the universe gives me hope for the present and the future (Jer. 29:11). The power to overcome the hardships I encounter in life, not all of them necessarily related to my disability, comes from knowing Jesus Christ and knowing He is in ultimate control.

My experience with God's abiding power helps me reach out to those who are hurting and to comfort them as my Lord and my friends comfort me. My disability is not an excuse for lesser service. After all, everybody has a unique blend of abilities and talents, along with their inabilities and weaknesses. Like the boy in the Bible with the few loaves and fishes, little becomes much when you choose to place it in the Master's hand.

Helpful Hints (when you meet someone with a disability):

- Speak to us age-appropriately (if the person is an adult, speak to them as such; if they are ten years old, speak to them as you would to a ten-year-old).

- Offer to help, but leave us the opportunity to do it ourselves if we can.

- Don't scold your children for staring. That gives them the impression there is something wrong with us. Take them over to the person and let them chat for a minute. It will help your kids—and you—to be at ease.

- To get over the fear of initial contact, take little steps. Introduce yourself. Try volunteering in a care home. Offer to do errands for someone, or offer to meet them at the mall. Stop and chat when you see someone waiting.

- When speaking to someone, try to either sit at eye level or stand a few steps away so they don't get a sore neck looking up at you! And don't be afraid to touch them.

- Don't assume a person with a disability is hard of hearing, or "not all there." Even if they cannot speak, there is someone inside that would love to come out if you take the time.

- We all have something to offer in this life; if you take a step in getting to know us, there's no telling what you might receive.

■ ■ ■

A prayer, found on the fly leaf of a Bible belonging to a missionary who died in China, found its way into my Bible. I identified with it many times, and in recent years saw in it a picture of Bernice's struggles.

> *Laid on Thine altar, O my Lord divine,*
> *Accept this gift today for Jesus' sake.*
> *I have no jewels to adorn Thy shrine,*
> *Nor any world famed sacrifice to make;*
> *But here I bring within my trembling hand*
> *This will of mine, a thing that seemeth small...*
> *And Thou alone, O Lord, canst understand*
> *How when I yield Thee this I yield mine all.*
> *Hidden therein Thy searching eye can see*
> *Struggles of passion, visions of delight;*
> *All that I have, or am, or fain would be;*
> *Deep loves, fond hopes, and longings infinite,*
> *It hath been wet with tears, and dimmed with sighs,*
> *Clenched in my grasp 'til beauty hath it none!*
> *Now from Thy footstool where it vanquished lies,*

The prayer ascendeth... may Thy will be done!
Take it, O Father, ere my courage fail,
And merge it so in Thine own will that e'en
If in some desperate hour my cries prevail,
And Thou give back my gift, it may have been
So changed, so purified, so fair have grown,
So one with Thee, so filled with peace divine,
I may not know or feel it as mine own,
But gaining back my will may find it Thine.

■ ■ ■

Bernice. Her name means "victorious," and so she overcame and survived the tests along the way. That doesn't mean she never experienced discouragement, disappointment, depression or doubt. Such times were shared with Jesus, sometimes with me, occasionally with a friend and often with the computer. She fought her way up from these low plateaus by standing on the promises of God. She related to Job and David in their times of darkness.

"Job arose, and rent his mantle, and shaved his head, and fell down upon the ground, and worshiped, and said... the Lord gave, and the Lord hath taken away; blessed be the name of the Lord" (Job 1:20-21).

"I waited patiently for the Lord; and he inclined unto me, and heard my cry. He brought me up also out of an horrible pit, out of the miry clay, and set my feet upon a rock, and established my goings" (Ps. 40:1-2).

"Better men than I," Bernice said, "have experienced darkness of soul, and have overcome in the name of the Lord."

Her sense of humour often came to the fore to help her make sense of it all.

"Sometimes life is like a game of Monopoly. Have you ever felt like you've just landed on 'Chance' and your card reads: 'Go to jail. Go directly to jail. Do not pass go. Do not collect $200'? What a downer. Everything had been going so well, but now...

"I was going through a time of real struggle, giving in to self-pity and gloom, trapped in prison bars of my own making. True, my disability was laid upon me, but being miserable about it is a matter of choice. Jesus, You who promised to bear our sorrows, lift the other end of the yoke, the heavy end.

"It's hard to express your feelings when you don't understand them yourself. What do my emotions reveal? Confusion? Loneliness? Guilt? Insecurity? I don't understand. Why do I feel this way? Is it wrong? Analysis of my thoughts does not come easily. Is it natural or unnatural? Does it show spiritual immaturity? What is it that seems to come between me and peace with God? Show me, Lord. Help me. 'Restore unto me the joy of Your salvation.' Help me understand myself and what I'm going through. Is it spiritual adolescence? There is victory in Jesus, I know. Help me 'soar on wings like eagles' above it all. The transformation happening within hurts at times, but I am confident that with Your help, I can burst forth as a butterfly... a new person. But now I need Your touch, Your strength, to see me through. Thank You, Lord."

Bernice emerged from that gloom, that spiritual adolescence as she called it, into the joy of the Lord again. But she discovered, as all pilgrims do, that the battle is not over until we reach the Celestial City. For there is a perverse principle operating within us, as we read in Romans 7:21-24, NIV, "So I find this law at work (in me): When I want to do good, evil is right there with me. For in my inner being I delight in God's law; but I see another law at work in the members of my body, waging war against the law of my mind and making me a prisoner of the law of sin at work within my members. What a wretched man I am! Who will rescue me from this body of death?"

Can this be the Apostle Paul speaking, a man chosen and equipped by the Lord to take the gospel to the Gentiles (Acts 9:15)? We are all frail flesh, even Paul. We carry the grace of God in clay pots. But that grace is sufficient for us, as Paul himself affirmed in Romans 8: "The law of the Spirit of life in Christ Jesus hath made me free from the law of sin and death," and "there is therefore now no condemnation!" (Rom. 8:1-2). Praise God!

We proceed on the journey, aware that we may encounter valleys, and occasionally the "slough of despond," but confident that the outcome is assured, for the Lord has promised to "keep you from falling, and to present you faultless before the presence of His glory with exceeding joy" (Jude 24).

We wait for that final redemption when the soul is delivered from its handicap, both physical and spiritual.

That deep-seated faith in the promises of God came to the rescue many times. The following entry in Bernice's journal relates a particularly poignant period of discouragement.

I Exist

Entrapped by an outer shell
That keeps me from being free,
Physically speaking.
Yet deep inside the real me should be free.

The God I love has promised that.
My spirit wings are hanging limp.
I'm told to soar as an eagle
High above my problems.
Somehow this life, this 'jail'...
Has taken away my ability to fly.

God has a purpose for your life I'm told.
But I've no destination, other than heaven,
Some day.
No goals to strive for,
Other than His will.
I know not whether I walk with Him
Or am lost in the forest of self-will.

I fill my mind with knowledge...
Courses on this and that,
But I never really get anywhere.
It's like walking on a treadmill.
Or groping in the dark.
I spend hours upon hours compiling a book,
A book the editors say is not original enough.
"There is nothing new under the sun?"
My autobiography is no different.
I can't shape my words
So people will want to read it.
Oh, God, I want to reach folks with my experience,
But I can't.
I have no ambition, no enthusiasm
To keep on.

With work, anyone can write, I'm told.

I'm only fooling myself.
How can a nobody
From an unknown village
Expect to storm the world
With a message of hope?
It's impossible. It's stupid.

Yet God loves to choose
The weak and impossible people
As agents for His miracles.
Shall I give up?
Are you kidding?
I'm on the edge of a personal earthquake.
God is going to shake me up
Until I realize that HE IS ABLE.

The biggest miracle to occur
Is not my body being made straight,
But my warped attitude being released
To victory and joy and hope.

The hope is that someday
I'll wrap myself in a cocoon
And come out with wings.
My spirit is growing wings now.
But soon my body will be free too.
Whether that will be here or hereafter
Only God knows.

"But until then I will sing with
joy in my heart."
With JOY?

Yes, Bernice.
The sun still shines to warm my heart,
Not from the outside, for the sky is cloudy,
But from the inside the SON'S rays
Of comfort and love
Radiate to make my spirit glow.
His Spirit charges my spirit with the electricity
Of eternal life.
God, never let me lose touch with that SOURCE.
YOU.

Broken Vessels, Leaking Cisterns

Lord, we feel like life has crushed us
Into shattered bits of clay
And our worn-out, leaking cisterns
Hold no water, though we pray
For You to mend the cracks, and
Put the pieces back in place...
But nothing seems to happen
Though we seek Your healing grace.
No oil is in our vessels,
Our cisterns are almost dry;
New cracks and broken pieces show
As troubles multiply.
Oh Lord, we seek You earnestly
If You don't intervene,
Our spirits soon will wither
From lack of heaven's rain.

"My child, you are so blinded,
You cannot see My hand
Remaking every piece of clay.

Oh, try to understand.
I can't just mend your vessel, or
Fill the cracks so they won't leak
Because the fiery kiln of testing
Would prove that vessel weak.
The seams would not be strong enough
And soon you'd break again.
No, that is not My purpose.
What is the answer, then?
You must be very willing
To allow what are My plans
And give your all completely
To the Master Potter's hands.
For you think you now are broken,
But you must be broken more;
Your vessels must be flattened
In humility before
I start right from the ashes
To build up something new.
The vessel of My choosing,
The brand new, Christ-like you!
My Son Jesus is the model
I work with through the years,
Inlaid with "gold," well purified
Through the furnace, through the tears.
Every vessel fit for service
Hangs on tough through every turn
As I remake My children
Into precious, priceless urns."

The worn-out, leaky cisterns
Can be changed the self-same way,

Transformed to new and perfect
As the Potter forms the clay.
Most carefully He builds them
With no scars or weakened wall;
If an imperfection rises,
He replaces one and all.
And speaks to reassure us
That though troubles seem to last,
To hold unto God's promise
Till the day when life has passed.
Then forever we will reign with Him
(Who formed us here below)
In heaven, clean and perfect.
Until then, we'll never know
What blessings are in store for us
Who serve the Lord today
But every trial and testing
Will be worth it all someday.

"...The sufferings of this present time are not worthy to be compared with the glory which shall be revealed to us" (Rom. 8:18).

—*Bernice Boyes*

CHAPTER TWELVE

Seeing the Promised Land

In the early months of 1995, Bernice's writing became more contemplative, looking inward to that secret place of communion and fellowship with the Lord; looking forward to that place which "eye has not seen, nor ear heard, neither have entered into the heart of man, the things which God hath prepared for them that love Him" (1 Cor. 2:9).

Winter months can be grey and drab. She missed Connie. Shawn and Cheryl had moved to Vancouver, but Tim and Darlene were back in Regina. Praise the Lord! As the weather improved, she found reasons to come home for visits. Grace Tubello designated a weekend or two to the northern trek. On other occasions, the STC accessible bus delivered her almost to the door.

She arranged to be home for her birthday in April; in June, just for fun... to connect with Aunt Sue's visit in Saskatoon a little later, and in September, for my birthday.

On these occasions we enjoyed coffee parties with friends, Kathy, Pam and Shelley, aunts and uncles, neighbours from near and far... just to touch base and recall good times.

We noticed over the summer that Bernice seemed to tire more easily. A persistent cough had developed in the spring. Apparently not related to a cold, it was particularly distressing at night. We called our old friend Dr. Gerrard, now retired, to ask his opinion. He suggested that due to her extremely calcified torso, her stomach would be squeezed into an elongated shape. It is possible, he said, that when she lies down, stomach acids are pushed into the esophagus, causing irritation. He suggested raising the head of the bed. A WRC doctor arranged for a bed with adjustable positions. It helped a little. We were concerned about loss of sleep and that one foot appeared to be swollen. Fear raised its head again. Noting her list of "fear not" promises on the wall, we asked the Lord for wisdom to know how to proceed.

Disturbed nights notwithstanding, once she was up and dressed, hair arranged, a touch of blush added and coffee in hand, she was ready to face the day and its responsibilities. Often, I would be sitting in the dining area waiting for her, listening for the hum of the wheelchair coming down the hall. As she rounded the corner, looking good, my heart leaped a little with a strange, emotional mixture of relief, love, anxiety, happiness and hope.

Together we set about tackling some of the duties on her priority list. One of them, November's Crafty Creations sale, loomed on the horizon. Since we learned so much from last year's successful venture, our planning proceeded smoothly. I stayed with the Harkers and spent each day helping Bernice do whatever seemed most urgent.

As the day arrived, all hands reported for duty. If the body flagged under fire, nothing was said. The excitement of seeing crafters and customers busily engaged in transactions energized us all. Bernice drew early shift on Saturday. I helped her dress and found a cup of coffee to get her going. We put our hands and heads together to ask God's help for the day, then went to work.

Jack produced hot muffins and coffee for those who missed breakfast while Bernice settled for a can of Ensure as she cruised about, a sweet, smiling trouble-shooter. We strolled past the organ man, Ken Rodenbush, making music in his corner, for our "fix" of serenity and peace. *Play it again, Ken.* We went shopping. Bernice found a festively decorated mail box on a stand, ready for Christmas mail. When Jil came along, we gathered our purchases and retired to Bernice's room for a rest.

As the day wore on, Bernice looked pale and tired, but did not complain. My feet were "killing me," as the saying goes, and I did complain. Just as the sale closed, Brian and Lily Stiller walked in. They had come for the Grey Cup game in Regina on Sunday, and called in to see Bernice. She, apparently, had prior knowledge of their intention to see the game, and keenly anticipated a visit. She posed for pictures with them, then gave them a tour of the building.

After they left, we realized we had missed the supper hour. Bernice ordered Kentucky Fried Chicken, which we ate in the dining room. I cut up the white meat for her and added jam to the buttered bun. We were almost too exhausted to eat. But her eyes lit up as she recalled the renewed contact with the Stillers.

"I wasn't exactly sparkling company," she admitted, "maybe even dull. But they understood we'd had a busy day. I'm glad they called. Imagine coming all the way from Toronto to watch a game and freeze! That's a dedicated sportsman. No doubt he had other appointments. Hey, maybe I was one of them!"

Bernice considered herself a bit of a football fan, too. She has photos of herself surrounded by muscled men in Saskatchewan green. If given the opportunity, she displayed a huge T-shirt boasting the signatures of Dave Ridgway, Jeff Fairholm and Dave Pitcher.

We recuperated sufficiently to attend church on Sunday, and later in the afternoon we got together with Jil and her parents to evaluate the weekend's events. They congratulated themselves on a job well done, including the crew of volunteers. I went to Brown's on the bus that evening, intending to be back early on Monday. Countless trips had made me a confident connoisseur of bus schedules. In the summer, of course, my car came into its own.

Yes, the car, my trusty Ford Taurus. We made many trips between Birch Hills and Regina, often with Bernice on board, stopping for lunch at Watson or Raymore, finally heading down Albert Street to 23rd Avenue. *Thank You, Lord, for friends who sometimes lent moral support by travelling with us. Thank You, too, for giving me courage to travel alone.* One summer night I slept in the car in the WRC parking lot to give me an early start on the way home. That's the time to experience early morning magic, to hear the robin's waking song.

Monday. Browns went to Saskatoon to visit their daughter, leaving a key with me as usual. "Make yourself at home," they urged. Bernice and I spent the morning doing catch-up jobs. Agnes Wolfe's letter from India had arrived. "Shall we work on that, Bernice?" The prospect of typing and photocopying seemed to daunt her. I offered to take it home with me. "No," she said, "I'll get to it later. Let's go for coffee."

For the afternoon she had booked the Para-transit bus to take us to the mall where we met Grace for coffee. We picked up some vitamins, window-shopped around the mall for a while, then went home. Bernice wanted to lie down, so we closed the door to talk to God and hear from Him. We reviewed her "fear not" exhortations. *Yes, we hear You, Lord, but this human heart with its apprehensions is hard to rein in.*

We ate supper in her room, with taped music in the background. Later, she walked me to the front door to wait for my bus.

Tuesday. I planned to catch the bus to Birch Hills that afternoon. We organized the mailing list for Wolfe's letter in the morning, and after lunch and a rest, Bernice prepared for her Bible study with the residents later that afternoon. I rounded up those in manual wheelchairs and helped distribute Bibles. My contribution in sharing something from Bernice's diary elicited a rebuke from Randy and Joe.

"You read her diary? How could you? That's not polite."

Properly chastened, I admitted my error. Those who are dependent on others for every activity and function of their lives have so little privacy. Only their thoughts are sacred to themselves. If we are privileged to share in those struggles and dreams, it is an honour to be kept in trust. My trust fund is full of precious, intimate memories.

Bernice accompanied me to the door to wait for the taxi.

"I'll just go home and rest up a bit, Bernice. I'll come back in a few days so we can attend to that mailing list."

"You could rest up at the Browns," she suggested gently.

"Oh, no, I need some clean clothes anyway."

The taxi arrived. I didn't kiss her because my throat felt a little raw and irritated. How could I know this would be the last time we would communicate face to face? In my mind I still see her in the wheelchair, waving at me through the wide glass doors. That memory turns a knife in my heart over and over. Hindsight has a way of focusing the mind on the essentials of life. May God, who directs His plans from the long range viewpoint of eternity, forgive me. When Bernice and I meet again, all will be clear to our newly enlightened minds. All will be forgiven, for there will be no sorrow there.

Wednesday. We talked on the phone. "I'm going to Tim and Darlene's for Bible study tonight."

"It's awfully cold, Bernice. Maybe you should stay home and keep warm."

"I want to go, Mom."

Thursday. We talked again. Bernice had an appointment the next day. She sounded a little doubtful about keeping it. Again, my sensitivity mechanism failed me. Did I not detect a little weariness in her voice? She seldom complained. Indeed, the next morning when she asked to be taken to emergency she told the nurse not to call me. "Mom will worry," she said. She fully expected the doctor to take care of the problem and she would return.

Friday morning early the doctor called. "We have your daughter, Bernice, here. She is not breathing."

Alarm bells in my heart. "What can you do for her?"

"We are trying. She may have aspirated something. We're having difficulty clearing it. She doesn't respond to our efforts."

Continued alarm bells. "Please do the best you can. Be gentle with her. I will come as soon as possible."

Dear Jesus, how can those small, restricted lungs endure this trauma? Help, Lord.

I asked the Browns to go to be with her, someone of family to stand by with love. Aunt Margaret, struggling with illness herself, never failed to be tenderhearted.

Millie Rowluck arrived with the car and we set off on that dark, blustery November morning, heading for Regina, four hours away. My heart raced ahead, with desperate yearning and foreboding.

You have intervened for her before, Lord. Would You do it again? We give her to You, the Great Physician. Work Your healing power as only You can. And if not? What shall I do if not? Can I bear to see her dear, familiar form when the light has gone out of her eyes, and I shall never hear her cheerful voice again? Images of her room, Main 5, and many friendly faces flashed through my mind. Dare I contemplate the prospect of a funeral? No, it was too much to fit into the cramped space of my overloaded mind. I asked God for direction and peace.

Slowly the fire doors closed in the back rooms of my mind, containing emotions too hot to handle, leaving space and time for what lay immediately ahead.

The information clerk at Regina General Hospital directed us to emergency. *It's true then, Heavenly Father, that You have called Your daughter home to heaven.* The doctor was sorry she could not be revived. He said we could see her. In that dimly lit room we found her, lying on a stretcher as if asleep. Only three days ago she had waved good-bye to me at the door. I kissed her and hugged her, still warm under the covers, her hands clasped as usual. *Farewell, my sweetheart. We shall meet again.* We wondered then, as we stood beside her, if her spirit, so recently released from the body, still lingered nearby, perhaps aware of us, before departing for her heavenly destiny. We felt somehow comforted by that thought. She is free now, in a way that we who are still confined to the body can only wonder about and wait.

■ ■ ■

At the Wascana Rehabilitation Centre we walked down the corridor to the Main 5 desk, to be met with stricken and stunned faces. In Jil's room, she and Sherry had contacted many individuals on Bernice's telephone list. We blended our tears and shared hugs, reaching for comfort, trying to comprehend what had happened. Disbelief was evident everywhere as people stopped to console. "We saw her in the elevator yesterday. She seemed OK. What happened?" One dear lady, pushing her mother's wheelchair, stopped to share a dream she had early that morning. "I saw Bernice standing before me. Her arms were stretched out toward me." Yes, indeed, she is now free of all restrictions.

Carol Oxelgren came to comfort. Flowers arrived from Connie's family and others. Dear Connie, so far away in Ottawa, grieving alone. She told me later that she had repeatedly called Bernice's number, just to hear her recorded voice, "Sorry, I cannot take your call right now, but...." This sudden parting for two close friends was very painful.

Sister Alice in Birch Hills arranged for MacKenzie's Funeral Home in Prince Albert to come for Bernice's body. For one unreasonable moment I felt an urge to ride with her in the hearse, so she wouldn't be alone. She's not alone. She's not there. She is with the Lord (2 Cor. 5:8), for so we are promised.

What a blessing to see Pastor Dave Wells and others from Harvest City Church. They were her family, her spiritual support for many years. He assured me he would like to have a part in her funeral and a memorial service. A WRC staff member, Bill Horbach, offered to work with Pastor Wells to arrange the memorial service the following Saturday. Bless his heart.

Bernice's room: so dear and familiar, now empty of life, yet everything in the room speaks of her. The nurse assured us that we need not feel any urgency to remove her belongings. We appreciated her thoughtfulness, but felt some pressure to return to Birch Hills to make funeral arrangements. Millie took a few bulky items home with her. Brian and Angie came. They and Uncle Jim could accommodate everything in two cars. Her wheelchairs and desk were left for others who would need them.

Sherry and Jil helped sort files. Material of significance to Resident's Council and SSILC were left for them. Boxes of files, binders and notebooks piled up, repositories of Bernice's thoughts over the years. Jil and Del kindly offered to retrieve material from the computer to be transferred to discs.

I pulled suitcases from the top shelf and began packing her clothes. Just last year we had packed, with great fanfare and enthusiasm, for her trip to Salem, Oregon, a high point in her life. Now these high-powered dreams had ended. We had faced death at close range before and experienced reprieve, but this time there was no turning back. She will never wear these clothes again. Remembering many shopping trips to Value Village and Sears brought a brief smile. Other, more unruly emotions clamored in the back rooms. Hot tears threatened, but the fire doors held fast.

We left room 529, Main 5 and the Wascana Rehabilitation Centre, a sad entourage winding its way back to Birch Hills, bearing my daughter's acquisitions of thirty-one years, while her body, that shell where she used to live, travelled another route. Her spirit had taken flight back to God who gave it (Eccl. 12:7).

Thinking of our load of things, now suddenly mundane and ordinary in the absence of the one who gave them worth and significance, my heart cried to God. "Do You see us here, heavenly Father? We are lonely and brokenhearted. We do not ask why anymore, for we know that all will be made clear some day. But we do ask, our Father, that Bernice's witness for You will continue through her writings; and that her faithful prayers will be gathered with those of the saints before the throne to be fragrantly effectual forever (Rev. 5:8), and that her many concerns for the well-being of others will continue to bear fruit. Those were her dreams, her life, her devotion to You, an offering. Receive them, Father, and make them a blessing. Thank You that you hear us. May Your Name be glorified."

Brian and Angie shared supper with me in Melfort. Food can comfort the soul too, as it fortifies the body. We talked and reminisced. My son and his family have been a bonus gift to us. Tom, married at 45, hardly dared hope to become a grandfather. He learned to know and appreciate two of his grandchildren before cancer took him at seventy-five. Brian and Angie's three children are a heritage from the Lord, to be upheld by prayer and love.

We stored our loads in Alice's spacious family room. After a cup of tea, Brian, Angie and the Browns, bless them, departed for Saskatoon. Grateful for Alice's hospitality, I collapsed on the sofa. Can this be a twelve-hour day? Have we experienced all this in one day? Just twenty-four hours ago I talked to Bernice. Now she has left us. Her room is empty. Her worldly possessions are piled in Alice's house. This is too much to comprehend. We talked and prayed and slept at intervals, preparing for the next day's responsibilities.

Pastor Olson of the local Lutheran Church offered counseling and practical guidance. The funeral, set for November 29, would be held in his church, more accessible to the cemetery. There, in Bethania Lutheran cemetery, Bernice would be laid to rest near her father, her grandparents, an uncle and other relatives. In the early days, that congregation, in true Christian spirit, had accepted us all in baptism, blessing and burial.

Brian and family arrived the evening before the funeral. We walked together to the funeral home to see Bernice's sweet face for the last time. The fire doors still held. I will cry later.

The funeral service, directed by the Holy Spirit, became an offering of worship to the glory of God. Familiar hymns from the Seeker songbook brought memories and tears.

What a day that will be
When my Jesus I shall see;

When I look upon His face,
The One who saved me by His grace.

—Jim Hill

Some glad morning when this life is o'er
I'll fly away.
To a home on God's celestial shore.
I'll fly away.

—Albert Brumley

Old friends from the Seeker group, Jack, Clifford, Gordon, Lewis, Fred and Don served as pallbearers. Many friends, present or not, carried her in their hearts, to a secluded spot in their memories to be treasured and kept.

Friends from the Baptist Church, Olive, Heather, Mona and Larry, shared their music. Pam offered a tribute to a friend who had not only survived her trials, but had overcome them with a victorious spirit.

But they that wait upon the Lord shall renew their strength; they shall mount up with wings as eagles; they shall run, and not be weary; they shall walk and not faint (Isa. 40:31).

Pastor Wells, who knew Bernice so intimately, spoke from his heart. "She became a valued member of our assembly," he said, "who taught us much of Christian grace and patience."

As Bernice would have wished, he spoke of her love for Jesus Christ, her Saviour and her deep concern that others would experience that saving grace. "In conclusion," he added, "I will let her speak for herself." He quoted from several of her writings, among them *All Things New*, the story of the caterpillar. That piece, written in 1995, clearly reveals her focus on that "better country."

ALL THINGS NEW

(As you read this, picture yourself as a caterpillar, seeing things as he would from his tiny world)

I am a caterpillar. My life is lived on this leaf, and as food supply necessitates, I will move on to neighbouring leaves. If I'm really adventuresome, I may travel to other twigs in the future, maybe even another branch. I've heard there is much more out there, but it is virtually impossible to envision a world beyond what I can see from my vantage point; not just other trees, but other forests and unimaginable beauteous things, colours beyond the shades of green and brown that I am accustomed to. Pools of water larger than the droplets of rain collecting on my leaf; innumerable creatures larger than the insects and other caterpillars of my world. Things I don't even have caterpillar-words to describe. Such a place it must be!

In time, I begin to feel the need to find a corner of my leaf, someplace where I can begin to grow a cocoon around myself. Instinctively, I sense something very different is happening to me. Life will never be the same. A new phase, a metamorphosis is occurring. But I don't understand what. Or why. Or exactly how my life will change. At first, I'm frightened at the shell closing in around me. I'd rather stay in my old world that I know, understand and enjoy. But then my Creator bathes me in peace and quietness as I await whatever lies before me. He assures me it is not the end of things, but the beginning. More than just receiving a new coat as He has given me before; a new body. I feel something peculiar happening to my physical being. I know I will not emerge the same. In the meantime, I anticipate with some trepidation. And hope.

Then, one day, the cocoon begins to break apart. A tiny hole at first, but it's a burst of fresh air to the dark, mustiness of my brief prison. I push my way through, opening the crack more and more. Brilliant light floods my view as I break past the final vestiges of my cocoon. I sit for a brief moment, perched on the threshold of a miracle, the familiar far behind me, but I feel no sadness. Everything has changed. I close my eyes and stretch out, cramped from such a confinement. A breeze catches me and suddenly I feel as if I'm floating. I open my eyes and realize I am! My new limbs are beautifully spread out beside me, holding me up in the wind currents as the world I only dreamed about before was suddenly being revealed around me. There seemed to be no end to the wonders, the magnificence. I could scarcely take it in. The greatest wonder of all was the inner knowing that my Creator had planned this transformation. Before I took my first step on my first leaf, He knew this was my destiny. I'd had such a narrow view of my existence during my time as a caterpillar. Now as I soar, I see the whole picture from my Creator's vantage point... and it blows me away! How could I ever have wished to stay as I was?!

Yes, I am this caterpillar. Life here and now is the leaf and twigs of my world. Rather than something to be feared or dreaded, death is merely the cocoon from which I will burst forth... into the splendour of heaven and the awesome presence of God Almighty which no mortal words can describe.

I will be this butterfly... my Saviour Jesus performs the metamorphosis.

■ ■ ■

When the perishable has been clothed with the imperishable, and the mortal with immortality, then the saying that is written will come true: "Death has been swallowed up in victory." ...But thanks be to God! He gives us the victory through our Lord Jesus Christ.
(1 Cor. 15:54,57, NIV)

Eye has not seen, nor ear heard, neither has it
entered into the heart of man, the things which God
hath prepared for them that love Him.
(1 Cor. 2:9)

And God shall wipe away all tears from their eyes;
and there shall be no more death, neither sorrow nor
crying, neither shall there be any more pain:
for the former things are passed away.
And He that sat upon the throne said,
"Behold, I (God) make *all things new.*"
(Rev. 21:4-5)

■ ■ ■

As we followed the casket from the church, Shelly, a
local friend, shared the taped song, "If You Could See Me
Now." Several of Bernice's close friends came to share our
sorrow. Tim, Darlene and Julie travelled with Pastor Wells
from Regina. Cheryl, nearly eight months pregnant,
arrived from Vancouver. One last time, on this side of
heaven, they clasped hands, two bonded hearts, separated
now for a while. Cheryl, her mom and Doreen Nichols
shared the trip from Saskatoon with Betty Dyck of Mail
Box Club days. Doug Powell, the faithful caregiver,
proved faithful to the final farewell.

As we stood by the grave side, shivering in the
November wind, it seemed almost comforting to see her
casket lowered into the sheltering earth. "From dust you
were created, to dust you shall return, and from the dust
you shall rise again" (Gen. 3:19; 1 Cor. 15).

First Corinthians 15 opens for us the astonishing,
mind-boggling prospect that though we die, we shall live

again. Jesus comforted Martha as she reached for hope
beyond the grave when her brother Lazarus died.

I am the resurrection and the life;
he who believes in me, though he die,
yet shall he live, and whoever
lives and believes in me shall never die.
Do you believe this?
(John 11:25-26, RSV)

I am standing upon the seashore.
A ship at my side spreads her white sails
to the morning breeze and starts for the blue ocean.
She is an object of beauty and strength,
and I stand and watch her until at length she hangs
like a speck of white cloud just where the sea and sky
come down to mingle with each other.
Then someone at my side says: "There! She's gone."
Gone where? Gone from my sight... that is all.
She is just as large in mast and hull and spar as she was
when she left my side, and just as able to bear her load
of living freight to the place of destination. Her diminished
size is in me, not in her; and just at the moment when
someone at my side says, "There! She's gone," there are
other eyes watching her coming, and other voices ready to
take up the glad shout, "There she comes!"
And that is Dying!

—Author Unknown

Taken from *Heaven* by Joni Eareckson Tada.
Used by permission of Zondervan Publishing House.

The Process of Grieving

After the funeral we gathered at our home to comfort one another and to share in the food provided by Angie and Brian. We were grateful for those who braved the winter weather to be with us. Emotionally on automatic pilot, I moved about, making all the appropriate responses, yet feeling detached from reality. Angie and Bettie cheered us all with refreshments and good humour, bless their hearts.

The following morning, still stunned and incredulous over the past days' events, we prepared to leave. Jim and Bettie planned to visit their parents, the Sundbos, at Caronport. I travelled with Jim and Margaret back to Regina for the memorial service at WRC on Saturday. A small circle of grieving family members, the Sundbos, Grays and Cousin Kathy, met at Browns for dinner that day.

We went together to WRC where Jil had arranged a table in the concourse displaying one of Bernice's water colours. I added her photo, with the memorial register. This room, so achingly familiar, the site of so many happy events, was now filled with wheelchairs, her fellow travellers here to bid her farewell. Glancing about the room, I spotted members of her Bible study group, WRC staff and many friends. It seemed that Bernice might suddenly appear around the corner. Would that I had one more chance to see and hold her. The fire doors and flood gates gave way at last. The tears came without restraint, comforting and healing. Strong hands clasped mine in empathy; voices, kind words and dear faces came to me through a blur of tears.

Pastor Wells again spoke from his heart, sharing the comforting promises of God. Dwayne and Joy Dalton translated those promises into music, a balm for the aching heart. Tim Miller prepared a tribute to Bernice. My heart is full of gratitude for these friends from Harvest City Church, who were so generous with their love and practical help, who came to grieve with us and comfort us. Other thoughtful folk had prepared coffee and dainties. Many thanks to Bill, Jil and Sherry for arranging the farewell. They are all family, as Bernice lived there for five years. They became a part of her life experience.

The next day we called at the bank to close Bernice's account. More tears. I still see her wheeling into her cubicle to use her PIN number, or when necessary on a shopping trip, finding an automated teller. The cashier was surprised and sorry. Sympathy activates the tear ducts. Other things too, countless things; places, people, situations and, yes, sometimes simply "things" brought memories into sharp and painful focus.

Early in 1996 I was asked to attend a memorial service

conducted by the WRC pastoral care department for those in their jurisdiction who had recently passed away. Margaret and Jim accompanied me. We sat with a few other bereaved families as names were read and red roses placed in their memory. BERNICE BOYES. *This is unreal. I was in this room with her for another function not long ago. Can this be happening?* Waves of sadness and loneliness washed over me. I sobbed uncontrollably. Others, chatting and drinking coffee, tried not to notice.

Later in the year, I was invited to the South Saskatchewan Independent Living Centre annual meeting, held in the WRC cafeteria. They had chosen Bernice as volunteer of the year and asked me to accept a citation in her place. Deeply moved by their appreciation of her efforts, I wanted to be there, yet was apprehensive at the prospect of close proximity to reminders and memories. Thank God, all went well. I heard a beautiful tribute to Bernice, enumerating her various endeavours for God and her fellow travellers. The plaque reads: "To Bernice Boyes... outstanding volunteer award for commitment and dedication towards the fulfillment of the independent living philosophy." *You would have been present at this meeting, Bernice. Are you aware of us?* It comforts me to think so.

Jil and company planned a craft sale again in the fall of 1996. For many obscure and indefinable reasons I wanted to be there... to help in Bernice's stead perhaps; to relive my last close associations with her. It was painful. Dear Sherry took me upstairs for coffee to allow me private cave-in time.

On Sunday, Grace invited me to Harvest City Church. We sat near the back but my eyes were drawn to the front row where Randy's bald head could be seen slumped over in his wheelchair. Nearby, conspicuously vacant, was the spot where Bernice and I once sat. I closed my eyes and wept silently. Heartaches. The old love songs expounded on them, but I never thought of it as real, physical pain. It is. It hurts. And there is no healing for it. It subsides and flares again. Time, they say, will help. It does smooth the raw edges, and memories, instead of being painful, in time take on a glow, like old gems.

Looking back on my first year without Bernice I marvel at the kind ministrations of my Lord, who so abundantly meted out strength and wisdom as needed. Spending Christmas with Brian's family allowed me freedom from the need to pretend, to measure up, to impress. Thanks, guys, for putting up with me.

Responsibilities awaited me at home; mountains of mail, letters to write, memorials to acknowledge. Sometime, somehow, I must deal with the boxes of things in Alice's basement. Where to begin? The mail seemed most urgent, and least stressful. Reading the cards, seeing the faces of dear friends and sensing their sympathy warmed my heart.

Accumulated stress began to manifest itself in physical symptoms: dizziness, heart palpitations, fainting spells. Alarmed, I felt sure something serious had developed in my body. Checkups revealed nothing noteworthy. Just the same, it might be wise to see my lawyer and "get my affairs in order." Sleepless nights only added to my apprehensions. I often phoned Alice to announce my intention to have a bath. In case I collapsed in the tub, I reasoned, someone should be aware. Alice and neighbour Del extended open invitations to sleep on the couch. These were pit stops on my journey back to normalcy.

I felt an urgency to do what must be done. I ordered a marker for Bernice's grave, determined to include the scripture text she had chosen, Philippians 1:20-21.

> *According to my earnest expectation*
> *and my hope, that in nothing I shall*
> *be ashamed, but that with all boldness,*
> *as always, so now also Christ shall*
> *be magnified in my body, whether*
> *it be by life, or by death. For to me*
> *to live is Christ, and to die is gain.*

What seemed like a commission from the Lord—to collect Bernice's poems and write her story—began to consume my thoughts. *Yes, Lord, I will do this, by Your enabling. Let me live long enough to finish it, Lord.*

Eventually, decisions had to be made about Bernice's clothes. I removed the name tags, sorted them and prepared to give them away. I discovered then what emotional incontinence means. I leaked at the eyes, often and without warning. So many intimate memories flooded my senses; the fragrance of her perfume, the jacket with coffee stains on the sleeve *(Oh, Mom, it just came back from the laundry yesterday!)* and many items reminiscent of countless shopping trips.

Bernice, you were taken in the prime of life. It didn't appear prime to many others, but to you life was exciting and full of hope. If only we could turn back the pages of time for another chance. But no, the plan you often spoke of led us here. One day we shall see it all, and understand. In the meantime we carry on, trusting the wisdom and kindness of our God.

There, in her room, surrounded by memories, I wept for her, thanked God for her and said good-bye. It cannot be called "closure," for the door isn't locked.

At any time a wind from the past can blow in, dropping a bittersweet remembrance, to be cradled briefly and sent on. Frank Sinatra's song, "I Thought of You," expresses that phenomenon. Everything reminds me of Bernice. Irrelevant things. A word conjures an instant flashback: Regina, Dewdney Ave., Galleria, Wascana, 33rd Street, Value Village. Simple activities like shopping and riding the STC bus are loaded with memories. Strangely though, the happy associations are more vivid and often elicit a chuckle or two.

I was drawn once again to a little clipping I found years and years ago, in which writer Doug Manning presented a vignette on grieving:

"A cut finger is numb before it bleeds, bleeds before it hurts, hurts until it begins to heal and forms a scab and itches until finally the scab is gone and only a small scar is left where once there was a wound."

Grief is the deepest wound you will ever have. Like a cut finger, it goes through stages and leaves a scar.

Bernice and I lived in each other's pockets, so to speak. She needed constant care, I was the caregiver. We were friends. We understood each other. We were on the same wavelength. I miss that close communion and fellowship. We prayed together, claiming the promise "where two shall agree" (Matt. 18:19). She possessed wisdom beyond her years. It has been said that an old person's death is like burning a library in that so much wisdom and knowledge is lost. An amazing fund of everyday wisdom, spiritual understanding, generosity and love is now out of our reach since you left us, Bernice. Thank God some of your thoughts are on paper and can be passed on. Much of your practical know-how still escapes me. Like the computer. And I still struggle with the simple task of recording TV programs. So quickly you passed me and left me amazed and proud.

Grieving and loneliness are common to us all. We deal with it in different ways. Canadian Prime Minister MacKenzie King had difficulty adjusting to his mother's death. He never married, and had been very close to her. F.A. McGregor, in his book, *The Fall and Rise of MacKenzie King*, calls him a religious mystic with a strong belief in life after death. Overcome with loneliness, he sought to establish communication with his mother's spirit. From my experience, I now find empathy for his pain. But while we are residents of planet earth, we are warned not to intrude into the spiritual dimension. It is the domain of hostile, satanic forces which control that great gulf which is fixed between us (Luke 16:26). The ancient King Saul, in desperation, sought counsel from the departed prophet Samuel. He was severely rebuked for this, and it proved to be the climax of his ongoing fall from grace (1 Sam. 28).

Through Jesus Christ, God bridged that huge gulf. He clothed Himself in human flesh to identify with us. He sacrificed Himself for our sins. He rose from the grave to give us hope of eternal life and sits in heaven to intercede for us. He not only promised to prepare a place for us with Him, but said that one day He would return to take us to heaven. Hallelujah! That is the real thing. Let your faith lay hold of this and find hope for your life's journey. Ancient Job asked the eternal question that burns in every heart: "If a man die, shall he live again?" Faith finds the answer: "I know that my redeemer liveth and He shall stand at the latter day upon the earth.... Whom I shall see for myself" (Job 14:14; 19:25).

Those who study grieving have observed that emotions range widely, and sometimes wildly, in expressions of denial, anger, remorse, guilt and depression. How can one deny the obvious? One could sincerely wish it were not so, but it is. Where should I direct my anger? Not at God, for as Job concluded, "...though He slay me, yet will I trust Him." The eternal God, all wise and all-knowing, has ways and means and reasons which are not explained to us. We'll trust Him until the day of revelation. Remorse and guilt? Yes. These weigh heavily upon me.

Why am I alive and Bernice is gone? She wanted to live. She had such hopes, such dreams and potential. At seventy-five, I am well and able to function. She reached only thirty-one. Is it my fault in some way that she was born with this strange disease? In my more sane moments I know this reasoning is not born of trust or faith, or even common sense. I consciously reject it.

Guilt and self-condemnation are persistent in their efforts to find fault and lay blame. Why did I not see the signs of Bernice's failing health? We worried about her cough, and tried various means to bring relief. She had trouble eating coarse food. Vitamin supplements helped a little. She seldom complained. She didn't want to worry me. I should have taken her home and arranged for a complete checkup with our own doctor. Perhaps I relied too much on the caregivers at WRC. They, too, in their busy schedule, in the absence of definite complaints, presumed all was well. Bernice was overly conscientious not to bother anyone. Only God knew her fears and apprehensions that last night when she called emergency. *Oh, God, I should have been there.* No amount of solace and reasoning can alter this fact. I failed her in her final hour of need. God, who is gracious, forgives. Bernice, sweet and gentle, always forgave. Where she is now, where all things are made plain, she has forgiven me. Forgiving myself will be more difficult.

Satan, our enemy, the "accuser of the brethren" (Rev. 12:10), continues to badger me with my failures. As in Job's day, he delights in pointing these out to God as well. But I have an advocate with the Father, Jesus Christ the righteous, who intercedes for me (1 John 2:1-2). "Who can lay anything to the charge of God's elect? It is God that justifieth" (Rom. 8:33). Praise His Name!

Can we by disobedience or negligence thwart or hinder God's purposes? Are His eternal intentions subject to our whims? Let us consider His long-range plan.

Back in eternity God said, "Let us make man in our image." The first Adam could not handle the discipline involved in free choice. He rebelled, but God pursued His original plan... to make man in His image. The plan now required redemption of the fallen creation. The second Adam, Jesus Christ the Son of God, was commissioned to become flesh and sacrifice Himself for rebellious humanity. In the meantime, God chose Abraham to head up a chosen people for His Name. Through Moses, God dispensed tough love on the long, tortuous journey via Egypt, the Red Sea and Sinai, which eventually led them to the promised land. In the promised land a star appeared one night, heralding the birth of a baby boy in Bethlehem. He was the second Adam, the redeemer and promised Messiah, Jesus Christ. He lived, taught, died and rose from the grave as planned.

Miles Stanford illuminates the overall purpose of God by pointing to Paul's writings: "As we have borne the image of the earthly (Adam) we shall also bear the image of the heavenly (Christ) (1 Cor. 15:49) and we know that all things work together for good to them that love God, to them who are the called according to His purpose. For whom He did foreknow, He also did predestinate to be conformed to the image of His Son (Rom. 8:28-29).

"Here," says Stanford, "is the good for which God is working all things together.... His original purpose of making us in His image, which is centered and expressed in His Son, Jesus Christ, who is our life. The open secret of healthy spiritual growth is to know and settle upon this fact as set forth in the foregoing scripture. When we see that all things are working together to make us more and more like the Lord Jesus, we will not be frustrated and upset when some of these 'things' are hard, difficult to understand, and often contain an element of death. We will be able to rest in our Lord Jesus and say to our Father, 'Thy will be done.' And our constant attitude of faith will be: 'Though He slay me, yet will I trust Him' (Job 13:15). This is our matriculation to spiritual maturity!"

—Miles J. Stanford

Taken from *Principles of Spiritual Growth*
Used by permission of Back to the Bible.

Through the ages, countless believers have been called to stand for their faith before a hostile world. Their names shine like beacons on the pages of history: Abraham, Moses, Esther, Paul, Augustine, Tyndale, Wycliffe, St. Francis, Luther, Wesley, Carey, Fanny Crosby, Finney, Susanna Wesley, Spurgeon, Moody, Graham. Other multitudes, known only to God and neighbours, serving Him in simple faith, casting their bread upon the waters in their own small circle, are being formed into the image of God. He who sees and knows all might be heard to observe: "Have you noticed my servant Bernice? I sent her into the world as my ambassador, to exemplify love, forgiveness, patience, servanthood and sacrifice. I allowed her to live with a 'thorn in the flesh' to help her learn these attributes. She accepted my assignment with grace. I recalled my ambassador after thirty-one years, upon completion of her duties."

Shall I continue to bemoan the brevity of her life? Shall I look for second causes in her death? God was not caught off guard by circumstances. No. Her duties completed, He called His ambassador home.

"For it is God which worketh in you both to will and to do of His good pleasure" (Phil. 2:13). And what is this "good pleasure" He is performing in us? He is working everything together for this one purpose: "That the life also of Jesus might be made manifest in our mortal flesh" (2 Cor. 4:11).

My beautiful daughter's earthly experience is accomplished. As the light of an expired star reaches ever outward into space, may the influence of Jesus' life in Bernice continue to bless in years to come.

Joni's Waltz

Though I spend my mortal lifetime in this chair,
I refuse to waste it living in despair.
And though others may receive
Gifts of healing, I believe
That He has given me a gift beyond compare...

For heaven is nearer to me,
And at times it is all I can see.
Sweet music I hear
Coming down to my ear;
And I know that it's playing for me.

For I am Christ the Saviour's own bride,
And redeemed I shall stand by His side.
He will say, "Shall we dance?"
And our endless romance
Will be worth all the tears I have cried.

I rejoice with him whose pain my Saviour heals.
And I weep with him who still his anguish feels.
But earthly joys and earthly tears
Are confined to earthly years,
And a greater good the Word of God reveals.

In this life we have a cross that we must bear;
A tiny part of Jesus' death that we can share.
And one day we'll lay it down,
For He has promised us a crown,
To which our suffering can never be compared.

—Nancy Honeytree

Taken from *Heaven* by Joni Erickson Tada.
Used by permission of Zondervan Publishing House.

Fibrodysplasia Ossificans Progressiva

D r. John Gerrard, Bernice's pediatrician, has provided an up-to-date review of her disease.

Fibrodysplasia ossificans progressiva (FOP) is a bizarre disorder in which affected persons are immobilized by progressive soft tissue ossification.

The name Myositis ossificans progressiva is said to have been assigned to this condition by Von Dusch in 1868. The designation in which fibrositis is substituted for myositis has been used more frequently in recent decades, since the primary change is in the connective tissues, specifically, the aponeuroses, fascia, and tendons, and the muscles are only secondarily affected. It is not entirely improper to refer to the condition as fibrositis, since the lesions may appear to be inflammatory during early stages. However, fibrodysplasia, the term suggested by Bauer and Bode, is probably the most valid.

Extraordinarily clear descriptions of the end stages of

the disease were provided by John Freke (1688-1756), a London surgeon, concerning a patient with FOP at St. Bartholomew's Hospital.

"April 14, 1736, there came a Boy of healthy Look and 14 years of age, to ask of us at the Hospital, what should be done to cure him of many large Swellings on his Back, which began about 3 Years since, and have continued to grow as large on many Parts as a Penny-loaf, particularly on the left side. They arise from all the vertebrae of the Neck, and reach down to the Os sacrum; they likewise arise from every Rib of his Body, as the Ramifications of Coral do, they make, as it were, a fixed bony Pair of Bodice."

Lutwak estimated that about 260 individuals with the condition had been documented up to 1963. In 1983, FOP was extensively reviewed by Michael Connor of Glasgow in his classic monograph, Soft Tissue Ossification. By 1990, about 600 cases could be identified in the world literature.

Fibrodysplasia ossificans progressiva is evident at birth in shortening of the great toes and to a lesser extent the thumbs. The condition is otherwise innocuous at this stage and may remain unrecognized until soft tissue ossification commences in late childhood.

In mid-childhood transient localized cystic swelling appear first in the subcutaneous tissues of the neck and back and late, in the limbs. Their development may be spontaneous or precipitated by trauma, and their resolution may be accompanied by a discharge of sero-sanguineous fluid. At times fever is associated with the tumors, and acute rheumatic fever may be simulated. As the swelling subsides, ectopic ossification forms at the affected sites. Bony bars and bridges cause progressive deformity and limitation of joint movement. Columns and plates of bone eventually replace the tendons, fascia, and ligaments. The spine may become completely rigid and maligned. A documented patient was unable to sit down... she was obliged to either lie down or stand up.

Stature and mentality are usually normal. The process of ectopic ossification slows in adulthood, but most persons with FOP are seriously handicapped by thirty years of age. The tongue, heart, diaphragm, abdominal wall, perineum, eyes and sphincter usually enjoy immunity from the process, but in later stages the muscles in the jaw may be restricted. Pneumonia is often the cause of death.

Unfortunately, recent studies of case histories have failed to turn up any definite leads as to cause or treatment.

CREDITS AND NOTES